Penguin Books

LAST FERRY TO MANLY

Jill Neville was born in Australia but went to Britain as an adolescent in the fifties, where she has worked as a copywriter, social worker, teacher, journalist and critic. Her literary criticism has appeared in *The Times Literary Supplement*, the *Sydney Morning Herald* and on the BBC. She writes a column for *The Sunday Times*. *Last Ferry to Manly* is her fifth novel.

LAST FERRY TO MANLY

JILL NEVILLE

PENGUIN BOOKS

Penguin Books Australia Ltd,
487 Maroondah Highway, P.O. Box 257
Ringwood, Victoria, 3134, Australia
Penguin Books Ltd,
Harmondsworth, Middlesex, England
Penguin Books,
40 West 23rd Street, New York, N.Y. 10010, U.S.A.
Penguin Books Canada Ltd,
2801 John Street, Markham, Ontario, Canada
Penguin Books (N.Z.) Ltd,
182-190 Wairau Road, Auckland 10, New Zealand

First published by Penguin Books Australia, 1984
Reprinted 1984

Copyright © Jill Neville, 1984

Typeset in Bembo Medium by Abb-Typesetting Pty Ltd

Made and printed in Australia by
Dominion Press-Hedges & Bell

CIP

Neville, Jill, 1932- .
Last ferry to Manly.

ISBN 0 14 007068 0.

I. Title.

A823'.3

CONTENTS

WASHED UP ON THE SHORE

ONE

The blue flaking ferry is rocking its way across the Harbour between the city and Manly, beyond the lighthouse and the furthest buoy, rolling so much you might be frightened that the sea will do more than trickle across the deck when it dips.

But no, it rises up, and just as well, for being the last ferry to Manly on a Saturday night it is full of drunks who would be confused by the roar of their drowning, mistaking the suction of the sea for their own alcoholic swaying. A few, though, are not drunk.

She saw her first naked man on a Sydney ferry. Aged fourteen, leaning too far over the engine, watching the pistons pump and pump, she had glimpsed a stoker stepping out of a shower below, in the hold. He had stood there, drying himself, her first Adam.

Now Bruiser is sitting opposite Lillian on the fake leather bench that has been ripped by a knife. He has not introduced

1

himself to her, and he wouldn't have minded the ripped bench even if he'd noticed it. Things like that don't count to him. They count to Lillian who has lived in places where money smoothed the edges of things and men in gleaming vans came gliding up gravel drives to mend the broken and maintain the perfect. What matters to Bruiser is his wardrobe: his clothes, the precision of the trouser folds, the order he has created with his blunt, tattooed hands.

One day Bruiser found a pair of shining shoes wedged between two rocks on the beach, a clue to some other universe. He has retained a passion for finding things and always walks with his head down, not to hide his face, as people presume, but just in case he spots a find.

An empty wine bottle rolls up and down on the wet planks, up and down in clattering echo to the roll of each wave rolling in from the Pacific. She stares at the rolling bottle and the dark dregs that seep out on to the wet deck.

Uneasy, Lillian is all in black as if mourning something. Nevertheless, she is reasonably slim and not too damaged by wear and tear. Even her hair maintains some of its Celtic red. Bruiser, the old dog, is on the alert.

At the airport this afternoon she had seen Bernard off. He was enraged. She had refused to return to London with him, as planned. 'Find yourself a woman you can love,' she had said, sensing the salty air at the end of the tunnel. His eyes came to a halt, with bricked-up rage.

Years earlier he had looked up at her, his head on her knee, while she stroked his forehead with the absent-mindedness of the Beloved, and the newborn blueness of his eyes should have made her afraid.

She reaches an arm through the window as if to touch a hovering gull. How fat their bellies are, these birds of prey. Her arm falls like a forgotten thing half out of the window, drenched, the silk-velvet ruined. Bruiser, the old beachcomber, wants to rescue it.

A reef-wave sends the boat tilting dangerously, and a man flops down on the top step, blinks, puts his bottle safely between his knees and continues to sing *Velia! Oh, Velia!* with histrionic longing. Underneath the light, blurred by an eerie sea-mist, a couple in evening dress returning from the Opera House are trying to concentrate on the small print in their programme.

Lillian is going to have to find a flat and a job, with no money (she could hardly put the bite on Bernard for money at the airport) and no contacts. The life-jackets are still stored under the seat. Blackened now with dust. Were they the same ones she had stared at all those years ago, before she left Sydney? She used to imagine the ship sinking, putting on one of those jackets, leaping wide-out into the water, making for the nearest rock, in terrible fear of the sharks gliding below.

I must make plans, she tells herself, as she plunges out on the deck into the wetness of the night and glares at South Head, grasping the slippery rail as the boat dips and rises.

On the other side of the cliff is The Gap. It is a part of Sydney where people who are planning suicide often choose to die. Sometimes a dog, kept there for that purpose, alerts the guards with his bark, and they drag the suicide back.

Bernard fancied that they chose to jump over The Gap because it faced Europe, Civilization. A neat idea, she supposed. But The Gap faces New Zealand.

'Hey lady, you're not gonna do anything silly, are you?' Bruiser bends towards her, holding the top of the doorway for balance.

Benign or malignant? It's as hard for her to tell as whether the shadows in the reeling sea are those of sharks or dolphins. A few black and grey hairs stick through his ruffled shirt. It looks professionally ironed.

She turns away and stares at the acid-green light snaking from the lighthouse. This is the harbour that once received the body of a drunken writer into its chill, deforming depths. He had fallen from this very rail, his pockets laden with beer bottles. A Sydney legend.

The captain is steering *The Baragoola* too close to the reef. They do odd manoeuvres on nights like this. It's as if the open sea is magnetic, drawing the ferry out through the narrow cervix of The Heads into the dangerous beckoning universe.

She looks down at the water. Strange he should think I was contemplating suicide. To splash in there, disturbing the reflections. What a stupid idea.

'Why don't you come in out of the rain?' Bruiser begs.

The sun is rising over South Steyne Surf Club, exciting the parrots into flashes of blue and crimson flight, squawking as if it's the first dawn they've ever seen needling through to their nests in the pines.

The rough sea last night left a wavy tide-line of bluebottles quivering in the brown seaweed, indigo bubbles with dark navy stings frilling the shore line.

Washed up a little further up the beach with the heavier drift-wood are two people. Lillian, still in her black coat, is lying on her side so that her hip takes on a lyre's shape. Bruiser is sitting upright beside her, adjusting the creases on his trousers.

He had told her, 'I'm a garbo. On the dawn shift. No point in sleeping.'

For hours she had sat beside him on a bench on the esplanade, staring ahead at the noisy sea. She refused to go indoors. The pine needles blew down around them. He kept brushing them off. But she let them remain where they fell, even in her hair. 'I've just left my husband. He's gone back to London.'

4

The sun, boiling with lights, stings her into moving, burying her fist in the sand, lifting it up, watching the shell particles escape through her fingers. She avoids looking at Bruiser's face in the light because of its impression of having been napalmed or cut up and stitched.

'I've always been called Bruiser. I used to wag school all the time, because of me bruises. Can't read or write now. Me wife tried to teach me. But then she had a baby. Went off me. Happens often, doesn't it?'

'Often,' Lillian says firmly, although it had been the opposite for her. He was a stray dog she couldn't get rid of.

A dero ambles on to the beach and spits in the surf, doing his morning ablutions, his quarter-full wine bottle glowing ruby in the rising sun.

Bruiser points out a peeling Edwardian building. Towels and surfboards are visible on every balcony. From the slope where they recline it looks as if the house rises straight out of the beach; a beach-shack. But there is an esplanade and a road between and a fish and chip shop, which also sells groceries, next door.

'It's not flash. But the joint below mine is going free. Them nurses are going back to New Zealand. They been fired. Kept taking sickies. Men comin' an' goin'.'

They stand up. She brushes the sand from her coat. On the esplanade a man is hosing the municipal marigolds. She pauses and stares at the parrots, newly exotic after so many years when the commonest birds were grey pigeons.

A jogger runs by, followed by a barking dog. The first cars appear. She promises to see about the empty flat below Bruiser. But first there are things to do. Letters to write. Packing. A hotel to leave. Money to worry about.

An old lady with a shamelessly withered body exercises calmly in her aged floral costume, and two old men with turtle heads stretch out their arms towards the sun.

5

Bruiser, child of alcoholics, ex-Metho drinker, goes upstairs to his flat to water his mother-in-law's tongue, the only plant to survive the scouring balcony winds. He opens his cupboard and gazes on his shimmering line up of trim shirts. Bruiser uses clothes, like some people use cream cakes, to shower attention on himself. But it's time to put on the overalls. He has been working for the council for years. Every day he sweeps up the pine needles from the esplanade. Every night the wind blows them down again.

On the front wall of Bruiser's house there's a small fading number-plate with a picture of a man dozing under a palm tree. It has lost one nail and rattles in the cruel beach wind. The door is held open with a stone and, as she enters the house for the first time, a gust of wind sends an empty Cola can skidding ahead of her down the hall.

The chipped wooden banisters and brown lino remind her of a house she'd once lived in, in World's End, London, where the door was always unlocked like this one. But never, in London, had she seen wet footprints gleaming on the lino.

One of the departing tenants is cleaning up, sweeping gusts of dust into the hall. Ruthless overhead light reveals buckled walls, mouldy carpets, a rusty pressed-tin ceiling.

'Want to have a look?' She is bland, blonde. 'Just getting rid of thousands of cockroaches. Five of us shared it. I'm the mug has to clean it.' There is no resentment in her voice.

Lillian looks past the bleached hair to the open door that leads to a bedroom and another open door and then to the balcony and then – it is like a Magritte trick-painting – the sea occupies the open doorway. She could rush along the corridor and jump into the sea.

As she steps towards the glint of water a surf-angel appears and hovers in the open doorway for an instant, his arms

6

akimbo, wide as wings. He has shot straight out of the blurred nowhere.

'Oh. *Surfies*. You'll get used to 'em. They practically fly in the bloody window.'

She follows the vision out through the sea-door and stands peering down on the narrow balcony. The sand at this hour has a city shabbiness, full of old crimes. The rearing surfer has become one of a dozen black shapes below, bobbing in their wet-suits near the rocks, taking advantage of the late hour, the clear, unpatrolled beach.

'You'll never get rid of the cockroaches, I'm warnin' you,' yells the nurse, now moving aside a bed to expose dust and an old red nightdress.

Lillian comes in and picks it up politely, but the nurse snatches it and hurls it up to the ceiling. 'Whee. I'm going home at last.' The nightie lands on top of a plywood cupboard with a rusty hinge. The door swings open.

The flat has a spermy look as if the nurses had been compensating on the side of life for working so much near death.

The walls bubble with damp, the lavatory seat only stays up with a piece of string and a hook. But nothing can put her off now. She plans to lie on that narrow bumpy bed that has seen so much roistering. She will stare at the sea, focusing on the furthest tip of North Curl Curl headland where every now and then a volcanic wave erupts to the very top, splitting the light into prisms.

'I like the flat. I'll take it.'

'It's old-fashioned.'

'I like old-fashioned places.'

'You'll soon start to whinge about it.'

She can't understand the agent's attitude. Is it her sex he

hates, her age, her European manner? Perhaps it's because she doesn't have a husband standing there, clubbing down her enthusiasms. He's thousands of kilometres away.

TWO

Lillian is relieved by the noisiness of the Manly house. It is so unjudging. The radios, thumps, voices and footfalls; the car honks and fog-horns; the mad noise of drunks shouting graffiti to the stars all increase her sense of privacy. There is too much going on for people to be much interested in her, not like the sneaky silence of the richer suburbs on the other side of the Harbour.

In the mornings through her bathroom window she hears the jocular voices of the Senior Surf Club men as they shower and dress in their locker-room next door. Sometimes, bending down to spit out toothpaste in the basin, she cannot avoid seeing a hairy limb or towelled flank. Never the heads. Those she'd see when they emerged to do their exercises on the front. Old men lying on their backs slowly lifting sinewy legs once covered in kisses; old ladies painfully trying to reach their distant knees.

At dusk the sudden racket of nesting parrots prevents her

9

from listening to music. She sits in the wind-rattled chair gazing at two Buddhists, their saffron robes billowing against a grey sky and sea so merged that there is, for an ambiguous moment, no horizon. Straight ahead the ships line up waiting their turn to enter the Harbour through The Heads.

From below comes the smell of herbal cooking or sudden running noises. In the backyard, where iron bedsteads rust inside broken shed doors, live two pretty girls. You don't have to go through the house to get there. It can be reached by a narrow side alley.

Young men go up and down that alley all day and night, their boards scraping against the walls.

Sometimes the couple downstairs emerge and do their Tai Chi dance. They look ethereal from a distance, but close up they have little, calculating eyes.

Next door the old man stares. He sits outside his house and intrudes on her with his gaping curiosity whenever she goes down to open the rusting letterbox.

'My next sweetie will come from the sea, like a mermaid,' Bruiser says to the old-timers by the wall who are used to his restlessness. He is looking again, they notice, towards the first-floor flat just underneath his own.

Earlier a woman had come out in a sarong and shaken a yellow towel. She had waved to Bruiser.

Now they see her again wearing jeans, half-lifting a bicycle out of the front door. She crosses the road and goes to the telephone box.

They stare at the bottom of her legs visible below the box. The jeans are shabby in the wrong way, and the thongs are old. The bicycle, they notice, is just an old coaster, no gears, nothing fancy.

The call over, she emerges, pretending she doesn't know

10

that she has the audience of old men, and begins to cycle northwards, swaying to avoid bins, dogs, benches, bubblers. In a shed a dero lies mumbling at the horizon.

A fan of gulls lifts and spreads at her approach. A white arc. 'That's the lady moved in below me,' Bruiser repeats to Ned, one of the other regulars by the wall.

'I seen her at the church jumble sale. Looks as if she's down on her luck.' Ned nods benignly. He had been in a Japanese prisoner-of-war camp. Like Bruiser, he goes every week to the Manly AA meetings on the hill.

'Bit of a sweetie. Never know your luck,' Bruiser perseveres. Ned nods and grunts; the sun feels like a mother-cat licking his neglected face. Bruiser is always looking for a woman.

The sun starts to get a stranglehold. Bruiser is enjoying the sunbathe, but he keeps an eye out for the boss. Once he'd caught him loafing when he should have been sweeping, and he'd been taken out of the open air and put on truck duty.

Soon he'll work his way down past Fairy Bower and clear out the French letters from under the lantana, then hose the toilets out by the pool and, maybe, sneak another dip. It was time the pool was drained and scraped. Terrible the things people did in that pool. Every time he went swimming he felt like the kids from the Far West Home up the road, seeing the sea for the first time.

The waves always shone for him with something of the same allure as Methylated Spirits had done. Destructive and visionary, they had possessed him with equal tenacity.

Now the beach megaphones high on their poles made their initial splutter, and a voice bellowed out: '*All surfboard riders are to move north beyond the flags. I said*, beyond the flags. *Otherwise surfboards will be impounded for one month.*'

Lillian pedals along the esplanade on her secondhand bike, the long shining line of the sea sliding away on her right. The waves are medium, but the surfers are out there nevertheless, waiting to enter their shimmering blue tunnels.

On the small of her back she feels the push of the wind. A man is blow-lamping paint from a beach shed, his hair blowing over his goggles. Oh, it had been worth it, breaking free.

A youth is lying on the grass on her left getting sprinkled with water every time the automatic hoses turn in his direction. He raises his head, gazes beseechingly at her, dribbles, holds up his arms to be lifted and rocked. She pedals ruthlessly away.

After a few metres she feels a remorseful pang. Years ago she would have stopped. Age hardened you.

She looks back nevertheless. The boy has his head right back as if inviting the sun to garotte him. Drugged. A piece of dead sea fruit washed up overnight. When you'd fallen through all the other sieves, this is where you landed.

Bruiser hopes this tenant will stay. Something permanent. That's what they need. Tenants always coming and going. He is the longest stayer in the house. Been there almost two years.

Now, whenever he sees Lillian on her balcony, he leans on his broom and gazes at her until she catches his eye and waves. Feeling encouraged, he spreads his arms out towards the sea in a proprietorial gesture. How can she rot up there in that damp box when all this is out here waiting for her? Misfortune had helped him get his priorities right.

When the ferry docks at Circular Quay, Lillian stares at the liner anchored opposite. Funny, she could still get that same old thrill staring at the big white liners bound for England. But it was better at night. The lights on the deck all glittering, the Harbour a wobbling tray of reflections, the stars humming with prophecies.

Lillian is early for her appointment. She gets off the bus and walks slowly through Chinatown. She remembers the Chinese community as tiny, shrivelled men covered with the centuries-old habit of resignation. Now their progeny are confident, full of sap, with direct, sparkling glances, their businesses thriving, their bodies tall.

Some bits of the city had not altered. Like the old tea merchant with his dusty crates and bags of tea. And the pub with its open door full of men from the market, chalking their pool sticks. And over all that old familiar Sydney smell of beer, rotting vegetables and melting tar. Men ambling along, jackets over their shoulders, shirts moist.

The sweat is starting to show on her upper lip, in the wetness of hair at the temples and in the kind of vacancy of expression women adopt when they are fanning themselves.

It was interesting to feel the wheels of life grinding on again. She had found a flat with a millionaire's view for fifty dollars a week and made an appointment with the editor of a daily newspaper.

Walking through the newsroom, aware of the hundreds of eyes on her, harpies in dark glasses preparing to demolish a possible new rival, she reaches up and snaps down her protective sunglasses.

'Australia is a good place to be at the moment,' the editor begins, as if making a public speech, eyeing her unpleasantly. He is a heavy, darkish man, the kind that normally excites her. But his mouth is prim, inquisitorial, as if he is permanently crossing out a misspelling.

Lillian sits in his office nodding with too much emphasis, a thing she does when she is uncomfortable. She knows he is a lackey of one of the newspaper barons, the most notorious.

'Of course, we can learn a lot from places like South Korea, the Philippines,' he says, gazing at her artfully. It was some kind of test. 'Their gross national production rises every year. GNP is what matters in this life.' She likes the pock marks on his bluish jowls. Men can get away with pock marks. Another of life's little unfairnesses.

She nods slowly, weightily. She hasn't done any international homework lately. 'It's a bit bothering, all those people getting executed on the slightest pretext. No adequate social security,' she says lightly, uncontentiously.

He pulls out one of the black hairs from the palm of his hand. 'I'm not saying they're perfect. They've got flaws.'

'You can say that again,' she chortles, thinking of all the Filipino girls who do anything to escape the degradations of Manila; marry any Australian they can find. She is embarrassed to note that her voice has taken on a worldly-wise madame-of-a-brothel note to mask her ignorance and suspicion.

'Do you intend to stay here now? You've been away for, how many years is it?'

'Seventeen,' she says, whittling it down a little. 'I've done work for all the London magazines.'

'I've seen your by-line.' Suddenly he gets up. 'We'll give you some freelance features, then put you on permanent casual if it works out. Our circulation rose a great deal the weekend we ran a supplement on male homosexuality. This is the second gay capital of the world, after San Francisco. Don't ask me why. It started as a prison, maybe they retained the habit.'

Lillian leans forward eagerly. She wants to gain the erotic attention of this burly bastard. 'I've never known such a gap between the sexes.'

The editor frowns irritably. 'I'd like you to do a three thousand-word feature on lesbians. They're taking over the city. Striding about in overalls; copying New York as usual, but without the panache.'

'I'm the wrong person for the job. I know nothing about lesbians.'

'That's what we want. The impartial view.'

She gets up, feeling old.

Just before closing time she wanders into the Botanical Gardens. There is no one else about. She is going down the steps towards the pond. But she hesitates for a moment and contemplates a Victorian statue of a chimneysweep, shivering in a London winter.

A derelict man comes up the steps towards her. His face is a gargoyle's, in the dusk. She backs up the steps. When she is in sight of the road, she waits by the fountain until he zig-zags out of the gates. An apparition from a horror movie. Tortured, doubtless, in his cradle.

She breathes in, then continues down towards the pool. She particularly wants to see the two statues of the nude women. The Bathers. They have been standing there, patiently looking at their own reflections, during all her years in England and France. She wants to touch them, touch their cool plaster arms.

At the bottom she can see the water glinting through the reeds. But the white statues are lying on the ground.

Both of The Bathers have been knocked off their plinths; the plaster rubble is still rolling on the ground, white dust is billowing. It must have been that dero with the gargoyle face.

She runs through the eerie grey emptiness, to the exit.

Smoke from a late barbecue weaves between scarlet and blue blooms. The Flame tree's erotic redness, the wounding blue of Jacarandas. Kookaburras laugh and dodge.

Out where the sea shimmers and adolescents flutter and twirl their boards like matadors' cloaks, girls with zinc cream on their noses wait, holding salty towels.

'What's it like in?' they ask, squinting up at a surfer returning, beaded in foam, his board on his shoulder like a hero's shield.

'*Unreal*.' That word they always use to describe the centre of reality in which they move. The girls have perfect bare breasts and the white blobs of zinc cream sit innocently on their noses.

When Lillian was their age on this beach, the boys had showed off by means of the high diving board, the back somersault and the divine swallow. Now, one boy, shorter than the others, comes towards her, holding his board. His eyes are noticeably dark, because he does not squint.

'Excuse me. Are you going to be here long?' he asks.

She lifts up an arm to shield her eyes from the glare; nods through the sun-dazzle.

'Will you mind my board? I've got to get to the bank.'

The sea-sprite needs a bank. She laughs. And agrees to be duenna to the board.

She notices a red mark around his ankle from the board-rope. His footsteps send up sprays of sand that stick to her oiled legs. She would like to strip and swim but feels ashamed of her body among all these gods and goddesses. So she lies down, and the sun soon knocks all thoughts out of her head.

When she wakes, the shadows have lengthened, and her legs are not in the sun. There's a silence of stupefied birds and no more smoke from the barbecue. She glances at her watch, brushes off shell particles, picks up her belongings. But won't leave the board to be stolen by the avaricious unemployed. She leaves a note pinned to the tree.

The thin, anxious woman with the reddish hair carries the surf-board awkwardly, putting her bare feet on the long shadow cast by the sea-wall. She had forgotten how scorching it gets in the late afternoon on the soles of bare feet.

How satisfying to go barefoot again. She will work on her feet until they are as insensitive as they had been when she walked on soft tar and sloshed through gutters turned into rapids by storms that burst after days of ballooning heat. In Europe she'd squashed them into shoes that always hurt. Now they looked almost as young as the surfer's.

I'm vain about my feet, she thinks, and then hears her mother's voice: 'A coquette's last refuge.'

She leans the board against a rock and picks some wild nasturtiums that grow all down the wet cliffside. Her father had told her how they'd had to eat nasturtium leaves in the Depression. How you get to like them. She inhales the smell of frangipanis, their odour of courtship and cheap dance-halls.

She picks a lantana and gazes deep into its thousand eyes; crushes it, inhales its acrid smell as homely as cod liver oil; picks a morning glory that will die in a flash, but not before she has outstared its yielding blue centre; thinking, When I was young, I was running too fast to notice flowers.

But she can remember, as immediate as her own heart-beat, those English springs; the first crocuses, like nipples, sprouting out of the iron earth. The parties people gave to keep themselves warm.

THREE

He lies down next to her. She smells coconut oil and something under that; deeply acceptable. He is prey, for man, woman, beast. Perhaps the board ploy was a dropped hanky; she was meant to rush after him, pleading for an assignation.

She raises herself with an effort and points over the road. 'See that grey house with the balconies. Your board is on the first floor. Come on, we'll go and get it.'

'I've got a flagon,' he says owlishly, showing her a half-empty flagon of white Riesling. Ah. So that is what causes the shimmer on the edge of his smile.

'I'll make you some coffee and sober you up.' She stands up and yells for the children to come, wraps a sarong around her waist, adjusts her sunglasses, holds out a towel for a running, shivering child.

She captures him and wraps him up. 'We wanna stay. We're swimming underwater.' His teeth are chattering in the midday sun. It's one of those days in which your eyelids aren't thick

18

enough to protect you from the glare. But the child's skin is turning blue.

'You've had enough.'

'We're playing a *game*!' he says indignantly, his eyes outraged, blood-shot.

'Well, don't go near the rocks, and watch those bluebottles. I'll only be a minute.' He rushes back to the foam to join his brother.

'I'm minding them for a neighbour.' She leads the surfer over the road. 'We'd better introduce ourselves.'

'I'm Simon, You're Lillian. I know that because I was at school with your nephew. Once when we were out there surfing we saw you ride by on a bike. He told me you were his Auntie Lillian from England. You'd run away when you were seventeen. Disappeared for twenty years.'

'Good God.'

In the flat flies buzz noisily. The squalor relaxes him. Anything grander might have kept him shy, subservient. He goes immediately to the magnetic balcony.

'You could dive into the sea from here!' he shouts. A yellow jeep cruises by. The bearded driver looks haggard. The boy ducks back inside. It's that ex-schoolteacher who's started following him everywhere.

When she stands in front of the coffee percolator, he brushes past her oily back, touching her. She recalls the bodies of the young girls on the beaches, yet concedes that their faces under the blobs of white zinc are the least interesting thing about them.

'Long ago, when I was sixteen, there used to be a high diving board here. I dived from the top tier and almost broke my back. That cured me of trying to show off with my swallow dive.' She gives him three slices of the cake she had bought for the neighbour's boys. Any friend of her nephew's, etcetera. But he refuses to be a Little Boy, ignoring cakes and old-age reminiscences and fills up her glass instead with deliberation.

19

She tries to forget his animal smell. The power of smell was enough to start wars, break homes, making children unhappy all over the world. Lately not having any other being to hug she had been intoxicated by her own muskiness, in love with herself.

'Are you jobless?' she asks brightly.

An embarrassed look steals over his face, which he attempts to dispel by means of his huge lit-up smile.

'I see. You're doing bugger-all. You want to be a dole-bludger for a while.'

He laughs relievedly. 'Have *you* got a job?' he asks, deflecting her question which, though well meaning, is authoritarian and has little to do with the contact behind the eyes, which is what he's interested in.

'Kind of. I freelance for newspapers. If I get sick there's no pay, though. No holiday pay, either.' Bustle. Bustle. She is bustling the words and the crockery.

'*You* won't get sick,' he says with intensity as if his slow-blinking eyes can see into her psyche.

'I don't want coffee,' he tells her and gives another roguish smile. Turning her back to switch off the percolator, she stifles a giggle. Her nephew's friend is flirting with her. The alcohol must have given him temporary myopia.

It has been a long time since she has seen skin with that burnished tan. All that soaring inside the crystal tube has matured him before his time. So many birth-traumas daily! Young body. Old soul.

Whatever it is, Simon, the eighteen-year-old veteran of a thousand such re-births and Lillian, avoiding the thought of being old enough to be his mother, sit in intimacy over a table where a puddle of Riesling winks back the reflection of his silver horoscope chain. She reads the salt packet. It is on the table next to the pepper packet. She cannot afford a salt or pepper-mill.

She stands up, shakes herself and runs out on to the balcony.

'God. I can't see them,' she yells. 'Let's hope they went back to their mother's. I'm supposed to be giving her a break.'

He grabs his board, leaving behind the half-full flagon.

He clatters after her down the stairs, his board banging the peeling walls and, after looking both ways in case the yellow jeep is on the prowl, goes his way, beachwards.

She enters the house next door, nodding to the old man in the yard, old Rumpelstiltskin. The roar and glare of the sea vanishes behind her as the door bangs shut. There's no open window anywhere to let in the air or let out the smells.

Up in the murky rooms she finds the children sitting with their tired mother at the kitchen table. Pinched little boys are wolfing biscuits. Their legs still covered in sand. Shirley, defeated-looking, with the mild eyes of the sacrificial lamb, is listening to loud pop music; its endless chanting about sex washes over her; loudly irrelevant.

'I'll take them back to the beach. I just had to go home for a minute and get something. Go and rest.'

She wants to return now to the beach, wants to get out there where the hefty men are wading in after their lifeboat practice, and the wind-surfers are skidding in arcs, and the coach-load of Japanese tourists are photographing the hairy barbarians and the sea is receiving all the pollution and pounding most of it clean again.

The Filipino wife fries another piece of fish for her.

'How are you, Merla? I saw some Filipino girls playing on the beach today. You must have been sweltering, frying in this weather.' Tears fill Merla's eyes.

Lillian puts her purse on the counter. And gazes hard at a plate of bruised pears.

21

FOUR

Bruiser is standing in her doorway holding an armful of shoes, the sea-light reflecting on his wrecked face. He looks down bashfully at his offerings.

'I came across this lot in the small hours. Clearing out them parking-lot bins. Almost new. Get a load of that.' He holds up a sandal so she can admire the pristine sole. 'Not a flamin' scratch. Makes yer wonder.'

'Just my size.' She slides her feet into a honky-tonk pair and knows she'll soon need plasters. She rises fifteen centimetres in height until she is on eye-level with his tender, blood-shot gaze.

'Reckoned they'd come in handy. Knew you wasn't too stuck up.' Tentatively, Bruiser steps over her threshold. 'You wouldn't credit what people leave behind 'em. Maybe they've been nicked.' He gives a wicked laugh. 'Maybe they fell off the back of a lorry.' He approaches closer. 'You don't feel crook or nothing. Taking secondhand things?'

She laughs the thought off with a blitheness mysterious to him. 'I don't have a thing to wear.'

Bruiser's face adopts a mournful look as if he's in the presence of tragedy. She wonders if she ought to tell him she walked out of a three-storey house stuffed with shoes, furniture, clothes, paintings, Georgian candlesticks and fish knives protected by green baize.

She's also left behind a husband and two sullen grown-up sons who had written to say that they had dyed their hair orange and green. Was it a semaphore message?

'Just between you and me,' he says, expanding somewhat, 'there's gonna be an empty flat below. Them hippies haven't paid their rent.'

He spills the shoes on her narrow bed. He stares at the thin blanket and dented pillow. There's a bobby-pin on the sheet. He picks it up and places it on the side-table.

She flings open the balcony door and moves towards the safe impersonality of the sea. He hovers near the bed but has to follow her in order to respond to her voice.

'I'll tell the family next door about the flat. They're all squashed together. It's awful. About seven beds in one room. The last time the old man had anyone living there must have been during the war. He rented it out for one-night stands to GIs and their molls.'

'There's always trouble there when people stay. And fleas. The old bloke gropes the women, too.' He has joined her on the balcony, away from the luscious shadows of the bed. She dismisses him easily out there, telling him she has to go to work. She's broke.

It's a small terrace house with a ship's mast lying in the front porch. A frangipani tree presses its branches like an entreaty against the side window. The door is opened by a small springy woman with untidy black hair.

23

'I'm Terry. We're all assembled. You'd better fasten your seat belt though.' She gives an old croaky laugh, but it doesn't have a malevolent edge to it.

Following her jerky walk down the hall, Lillian feels she's following a driven soul.

In the kitchen it's downhill all the way. Surreptitiously, she scribbles: 'Atmosphere – difficult.'

Overhead sways an unshaded bulb, bombarded by moths. On the walls are political posters, their subjects fascism and torture in South American countries. And land rights for Aborigines.

To get into the only empty chair she has to squeeze behind an emaciated woman who is eating bean-shoots, which appear to be growing all over the kitchen in empty yoghurt cartons. Everything is scoured clean.

On the wall she reads:

ADVICE TO A HETEROSEXUAL WOMAN
If you meet a Lesbian
Don't scream or panic.

Below this poster a hefty woman is plucking a guitar. She glances evilly at Lillian who thinks, Don't scream or panic.

Her girlfriend, a tall, prim-looking librarian, is gazing at this intruding reporter who will no doubt cheapen them for the mass media. Lillian glazes her eyes and makes a stab at general conversation. 'It's worrying, the information coming out about Aboriginal child brides, isn't it?'

'What's worrying about it?' asks the librarian.

'Well, all this work you radicals are doing to support the Aborigines and their traditional ways, yet, being feminists, it must bother you, the traditional way the Aborigines treated their females, breaking their hymens as infants, forcible congress with elders, and so on.'

'Where do you get your information from?'

24

'Anthropologists. Their books in the Mitchell Library and at the university.'

'*Male* anthropologists.'

'Not necessarily.'

'I think you'll find they are.'

They aren't going to be fobbed off with a paradox. She's with fanatics. She smiles her anachronistic false-approval and gets out her notebook and pen to mime getting down to business. They had agreed to the interview. She might as well get on with it.

'Your newspaper is not popular in this house,' warns Terry. 'It's disgusting the way that killer-bee who runs the show gets the poms to roll over on their backs and open their legs the minute he flashes his cheque book. He lies to them with affable Aussie cheek and gets away with it, every time.'

'Look on the bright side, girls. Here's your chance to state your case to the masses. Are you lesbians for political reasons or because it's fashionable or simply your nature?'

Terry rocks back and forth, emitting caws of laughter.

'Geez,' says the hefty one, laying aside her guitar with menacing slowness. 'Do we have to put up with this shit? Fashionable! In my home town it was bad enough if you were left-handed, let alone gay. And doesn't she know there's no such thing as nature. It's all conditioning?'

'Tell that to the lions and tigers!'

'Where's she been for the last ten years? In a beauty sleep?'

'I don't just bounce on and off bandwagons until I'm bruised, like some I could mention.'

'Stop squabbling! Let's get on with it! We agreed,' says Terry.

'You didn't tell us we'd have a patronizing pom.'

Lillian sighs deeply and concentrates on her overdraft.

'Have you ever been to bed with men?' she asks the librarian.

'Of course.'

'Did you enjoy that?' God, she thinks, the things I do to earn a dollar.

But she is interested in their bristling melancholy. Terry would obviously have been a lesbian anywhere in the world at any era; it was there in her ardent eyes. So would the hefty one. But the emaciated woman and the librarian look like uneasy new recruits. Perhaps she can work on them. But no, they are turning out to be the most virulent.

The librarian has picked up a jar of Vegemite and is ready to hurl it. 'What do you think? The usual ratshit. Up against the wall on a Saturday night. Then off to boast to their mates. Ugh.'

'Haven't you ever been with a man who's a careful, considerate lover; one who attracts you?'

'What point are you making?' says the guitarist. The emaciated one scuttles out of the room holding a bean-sprout carton. Terry looks amused, unthrown.

The librarian is aghast. Perhaps she has more to lose; there's the possible implication that she is embroiled with Hefty for lack of choice. 'Are you implying,' she seethes, 'that I'm a lesbian because I haven't been made love to properly by a man?' She could easily be the slightly hysterical wife of a country vicar; gawky in sprigged muslin.

Lillian is embarrassed by her insight.

'*You see*,' says the librarian, sinking back into the kitchen chair triumphantly. 'It's hopeless, talking to people like you. I told you, Terry. We can't trust anyone from that stinking newspaper. Look what they did to Whitlam. That bastard rag single-handedly destroyed him.'

'I'll vouch for Lillian,' Terry puts in suddenly and plonks a bottle of something called 'dry, flat red' on the table to divert the lynch-mob.

But the large woman with the guitar gives Lillian another look of suspicion.

26

'Did you get on with your father?' says Lillian.

'Look,' says Terry. 'Being a lesbian is a *positive* choice! It opens up the world. Like a fan. Not necessarily because of inept fathers or boyfriends. It just increases the options. All Eros needs is two people, and not necessarily a man and a woman.'

'I hope I'm not interrupting anything. I heard your typewriter banging away.' Simon is standing at her door, holding his board.

'It's okay. I need a break.' He walks through to the balcony where he parks his board, leaving sand tracks on the mat.

His visits now seem just all part of living on the sea-front, like the cacophony of bird noises in the pines at sunrise and sunset; the roar of the power-shovels clearing pollution and bluebottles from the sand each day; the stern instructions from the beach inspector on the megaphone – his endless admonitions to the surfers riding the wrong waves.

Wearing nothing but shorts, Simon is holding a flagon of Riesling as usual. Unemployment and surf-bliss drive him to drink. He'll have broken capillaries before he's twenty. He tells her about a man on the beach with a metal detector who has unearthed dozens of empty beer cans but no gold nuggets.

'Those kids next door are spellbound. They look pretty neglected to me.'

'Both parents are working.' She produces two glasses. 'Why don't you teach them to surf?'

He wriggles his shoulders in an escaping attitude. 'Too young. Do you like white or shall I bring red?'

'It's all plonk to me,' she says, spreading out the newspapers so they won't be burdened by conversation, or hurled into intimacy.

His limpidity. She is getting used to that. Like the presence of the sea on her doorstep. You can get used to anything. He is just beach flotsam, like the kids who come in to look at her shell collection, the deprived boys next door who break things in circuitous revenge for their uneasy home life; the white gulls which occasionally sit on her balcony hoping for a crumb.

FIVE

Sometimes on holiday weekends when the sun sends down red, hot nails and the littering tourists from the beachless parts of Sydney come over on *The Baragoola* in their hundreds, tides of trippers milling down The Corso, Lillian wishes she had escaped to the bushy mountains, to her remaining relatives there, fanning themselves on verandahs under the juniper tree.

On such a day, the dero might even rise from his perennial bench, amble over the sand and gaze intensely at the sea. Then spit in it again.

She had often seen his like sidling at dusk around the Botanical Gardens. But there were less of them about now; Sydney shamblers; flashing diseased and bluish penises like craven gifts.

During the week, between work bouts, she lies on her bed with the balcony door open, hypnotizing herself with the rhythms of the sea, feeling the tingle at the nape of her neck, pores opening in her very cranium. She can read thoughts, pick up the hum of dolphins. In the distance, a coil of white foam arches up into the sky, hitting the top of the cliff. You could never feel static, living near the sea.

Below on the esplanade the four doorless phone boxes are full. A girl is scratching her calf with a sandy foot, her young knees bony and innocent. The other occupants crouching in positions of entreaty or bravado eye her through the glass partitions, making endless contacts, endless conjectures.

A sea breeze ripples the pages of the phone books opposite, exposing a thousand names and addresses of people all waiting for a call. Lillian obeys the nudgings of providence and goes downstairs to ring people, to make something happen, anything, to fix up a few outings.

Terry's twenty-five footer skids out away from the flutter of other boats in the bay towards the last buoy by the reef where a long gull is perched, surveying the wild blue upheaval. In the sudden gusts from the Antarctic, Terry pulls her woollen cap further over her head, her leathery urchin face squinting up at the sky to deduce the wind's next move.

Lillian is frightened of the slippery deck and being beheaded by the boom, but bored in the queasy confines of the galley where she clutches a small boy in a tight embrace. She always seems to appropriate other people's small boys. Two more of Terry's acquaintances have also been invited out on her boat. That's how Terry deals with social life, with people who are neither lovers nor anarchists.

They are American deep-sea diving fanatics who have recently done a long stint of social work among starving Asians.

The couple look down hungrily at the sea shadows; glint signals to each other. Their sinewy bodies would soon be rounded by the sea; glide in and out of humming silences among schools of little striped fish.

Their son begins to whimper when the boat leaves The Heads and the huge waves seethe on all sides. 'I wanna go home.'

Lillian gives him a piece of polyester packing fibre to play with but longs to lie down on the bunk, pull the yellow curtains and doze until the day goes away.

When at last they are anchored in one of the octopus tentacles of the Harbour, Terry produces tea from a rocking spirit stove, and the athletic couple strap themselves into diving gear.

'Don't force him to go with you,' begs Lillian. 'Or to do heroic feats. He's not the type.'

They glare at her. From their lean athletic loins they have produced a son appalled by six metre waves and the deathly pessimism of Asian children starving to death all around him.

When they come in to dock, Terry gives the rope to Lillian, instructing her how to throw it over the bollard. She throws it and misses.

'Struth. Going out with your boyfriend?'

She twirls before him in a silver dress. 'Just a woman I had a letter of introduction to. A film producer. She's giving a dinner party.'

'You're having me on.' Bruiser holds up a brown cardigan, swaying it before her like the golden fleece. 'Cop a load of this.'

'Hand-knitted!'

'Found it in a flamin' bin. That's where the owner must be, silly berk, in a bin.' He laughs beseechingly.

'I'm late, Bruiser. Must dash.'

He looks away, not quickly enough to conceal the forlornness in his face.

She kisses the cardigan gratefully – easier to kiss than his wrecked face – and places it reverently on the hall-stand. She agrees to accompany him to his next AA meeting.

He walks along the esplanade in the opposite direction, in perfectly pressed trousers.

These rich Sydney women seem like caricatures to her, like drag queens, too insistent, too emphatic. And the less meaning their remarks have the more they emphasize them. The men are mainly homosexual, egging on the flamboyant females in order to recoil from them later.

The hostess is a jubilant Chaucerian woman, plump and dark. She devours the few attractive men with her eyes. Her venality is so shameless that flirtation would be a contest Lillian was bound to lose, unless she was prepared to wrestle for her prize.

Looming in a corner by the open fire, she counts thirty-four silver-framed photographs on the table.

'Known Jacky long?' asks a popinjay. His face is shaved so close his skin seems pre-pubescent. She always likes a bit of stubble; the escaped-prisoner look.

'No. I'm a friend of a friend.'

'Where do you live?' His eyes have gone dead already. The ashes of politeness.

'Manly.'

'Manly! You must be mad, dear. It's a slum.'

'But it's on the beach, and only fifteen minutes from town.'

'I couldn't live anywhere but the Eastern suburbs myself.'

She glances at her watch. It's only 8.30. Her face already feels sore from insincere grimaces. Now the room is filled with overdressed women with too few escorts.

It is one of those evenings that don't take off. At dinner Lillian listens to a flint-eyed man tell her how he abandoned advertising for the movie business, and someone thumps her on her left arm.

It is the butler, holding out a silver platter in his white-gloved hands, offering her more entrée. 'He thumped me on the arm!' she would tell people later. The Australian butler.

The hostess, endearingly honest, simply gives up and goes upstairs.

'I think our hostess has deserted us.'

'Nonsense. She'll be back. She's probably just checking on the children.'

When she doesn't return, Lillian says, 'We should all hire ourselves out as rent-a-boring dinner party.'

The disgruntled guests help themselves to food from the sideboard because the butler has also disappeared. Even the piped Mozart has been switched off.

Lillian goes upstairs in search of a lavatory and glimpses the ebullient hostess in her bedroom. Her dark hair is tumbling over her plump white shoulders. She is in deep embrace with a man, who may or may not be the butler.

Lillian walks out laughing to cruise the empty, silent streets for a taxi, inhaling the smell of jasmine. There is a ramshackle quality to both high and low society in her home town which she enjoys and now recognizes as an irredeemable part of her own make-up.

'Coming?' Bruiser is waiting for her, shining with what she is too self-deprecating to recognize immediately as pride. He almost struts. It isn't often that he's seen with a pretty woman.

Tactfully wearing the sandals he had found in the parking lot, she clatters downstairs behind him.

'New bloke moved in down here.'

'Yes, I glimpsed him, Bruiser. Funny, bulging blue eyes.'

'He's been through the Pacific,' Bruiser says reverently, exonerating him from any misdeed in advance. 'Why didn't yer mate Shirl from next door grab it?'

'Her husband is planning to move them all back to New Zealand.'

As they climb the cliff stairs the long garland of northern beaches interspersed with headlands unwinds below. Each beach has a different character, each headland a different flash of memory; a first kiss with a young musician while she stared at the flaw on a tomato; picnics smelling of boronia; chops falling into the fire; the old changing-room with the silvered mirrors; sliding screaming down sandhills into the Curl Curl lagoon, then dark blue and unpolluted.

Her mother had often spoken of the days before the developers tore down the Victorian buildings, when Sirius Cove had a dance-hall in the scrub, a trip to Palm Beach before the Spit Bridge was built was fraught with adventure and Pittwater was dotted with rickety old boatsheds that let in starlight between cracks.

Sometimes she saw the remains of that Sydney: the old wooden post office at Church Point near the spot where you could still hire dinghies; the dance-hall at Palm Beach now converted into a film studio, the slatted floor where she'd foxtrotted; and the main connection, the old *Baragoola*. Creaking along. A ship of ghosts.

'What happens at these meetings, Bruiser?'

'You don't have to do nothin'. You're a visitor. Just listen. You get a nice cuppa tea and a bikkie.'

The hall was set back from the road among pungent bushes blooming now with some hardy, prickly flower.

'Found a job yet?'

'Sort of.' She doesn't want to talk about it. And she doesn't want to talk about her family. Any more intimacy and he would be attached to her forever; a burr in her cardigan.

34

Bruiser isn't too forthcoming about his past, either. She has heard that he's been in prison, in an asylum, all the things that happen to you if you're born in the gutter.

At the hall over tea she is enlightened a little by Ned. Their faces, she notices, all have the same deep seams; alcoholic scars.

'Bruiser was a Metho man, wasn't you Bruiser. On the streets at ten, he was. By himself. What can you expect? Trouble with the cops.'

'I used to love me Metho. I used to get turned on just by . . .' Bruiser holds up an imaginary bottle 'just by gazin' at the flamin' picture of the skull-and-cross-bones on the label.'

'And look at him now. You wouldn't recognize him. In that gear. Flash as a rat with a gold tooth.'

During the meeting Lillian cries. She cries from the moment the first member stands up and starts his monologue:

'I didn't have a drink for eleven months, one week and three days, did I darling? Then I fell, made a pig of meself.'

A woman in the audience smiles up at him. Forgiveness cast its haggard shadow over her chipped face.

'After that I vowed "never again", and I've kept me word. It's been nearly five years now.'

Everyone claps. The tears gush up from the frozen lake inside her. She lifts herself off the hard chair, then sits down again. She is not an alcoholic. She has nothing to do with alcoholism.

When each alkie stands up to tell his story, she sobs. Go on, get it over with, confess, get it off your chest. You name it, I'll cry. She is wallowing in pity for the human condition; pity for herself, at one remove. She stuffs a handkerchief to her face, Bruiser's, of course.

'Day at a time,' quotes the last speaker, quoting from the AA handbook. 'If I can just get through this day as if it was my last day. I say that to myself every morning. And you know, it works folks. Otherwise you just sit about worrying.'

35

A final black sob explodes inside her. *Day at a time*. She'll try that.

'What was all that crying about?' Bruiser is walking her home.

'Oh, don't worry about it. I cry like that at the cinema, too.' Thin, factitious tears, perpetual rain in the darkness of the cinema.

When they come down the cliff steps, she walks along the sea-wall like the Manly children do, so that Bruiser isn't tempted to take her hand or anything.

It's Saturday night, night of purgings and awkward truths. Cars screech by still; a woman reels on the sand in the darkness sobbing or laughing. The sound of a Surf Club party jerks on the night wind. Boys with blank eyes and sarongs, goofily grinning, follow a girl with a frangipani blossom in her hair out to the dark beach.

Shirley from next door, usually so timid, knocks loudly. She is frightened, cradling the smallest of her boys. Lillian lets her slip inside for shelter, bolting the door behind her. She has the look of one being followed.

Before any explanations she tucks the child into her bed. In the kitchen Shirley is trembling violently. 'He's drunk. Put a gun in his mouth and said he was going to shoot himself. Made Andrew watch him.' Her voice whistles into a sob. 'The littlest slept through it all. But I've got to go back and get Andrew.'

'I'll come with you . . .'

'No. But if I'm not back in ten minutes, come then.'

Lillian tiptoes past the sleeping boy to keep watch on the house next door. Out on the beach a couple are embracing. From the Surf Club the sounds of the band are diminished by the rock of the sea. Soon the girl who had simulated sexual passion on the beach with a dozen surfers walks by as if sore, her frangipani brown and crushed, doing up her sarong. Her face is plain under the orange lights.

Shirley's husband emerges from the house, bends down to pick up a broken plank from the gutter. He lifts it high over his head, lets it crash down on to a white panel-van parked there, denting it at once.

Shirley smuggles in her eldest child. They put him on the sofa. But he lies there stiffly. His eyes are too small for a child's, sunk back into his head with the weight of things. Lillian tries stroking his rigid forehead, then gives him a banana, which he lets slip on to the floor.

He can hear his father smashing away at the panel-van, alerting the neighbourhood; splintering his heart.

'You're disturbing my wife,' shouts the tyrant from the shop, who approaches the source of the noise, doing up the cords of his orange dressing-gown.

'Call the cops,' shouts Rumpelstiltskin.

But Bruiser appears, soothes the tyrant, draws the sting from Rumpelstiltskin. No doubt he is explaining that Shirley's husband has been through the Pacific. But no, he can't use that magic charm. The man is too young.

'He's been nice and quiet for so long too,' says Shirley, crouching low by the balcony so she can't be spotted by the ogre still crashing timber against metal; avenging himself on the inanimate world.

'He's been paying off the HP for over a year. It's his pride and joy. I don't know what's got into him. It's that fibreglass factory. The stuff gets into his skin. Someone will call the cops.' She is keening.

'No. Bruiser put a stop to that. He told them that the phone boxes were out of order. And the next one is way up at The Corso.'

There's a new spectator, the tenant from below, the old soldier; his eyes red in the streetlights, responding to the sweet old music of combat.

'He's been that quiet,' she repeats. 'Hasn't gone out to the pub or nothing, for eight months. Just stays home and listens to the Top Ten.'

'Perhaps that's just the trouble,' Lillian says gently, then sits for a while near the bigger boy. His eyes are still open, small and very open. She sits next to him, holding his forearm while Shirley continues to watch the demolition.

'Don't forget, Andrew, that your Dad is mostly a good Dad,' soothes Lillian. 'He's just drunk. He doesn't know what he's doing.'

'Once,' the boy says dreamily, 'Daddy picked up a stone and threw it at Mummy. We were on a picnic.' The responsibility of allying himself with his father weighs heavily on him.

The noise bangs about for hours, like the empty tin cans rattling on asphalt, driven along by a southerly buster.

She can't sleep. She hears the dawn ferry. Its fog-horn baying out on a minor note that disturbs her. The past nudges at her mind; a sunken boat risen to the surface after a particularly violent storm; its barnacled hull gaping in the daylight.

It seems to be the appropriate time and place to be haunted, washed up.

Beached.

CASUALTIES OF ROMANCE

SIX

Chubby youth wanted, amenable to discipline.

Lillian, in leaking snowboots, scrutinized an ad further down the newsagent's window: *Bedsitting room to let. h & c. Gas ring. No pets. No coloureds. Quiet lady preferred.* Quiet lady preferred. No good. She would never be quiet enough. She might as well stay on in the old joint in World's End. She had shared it with Felicity before she went off and married on the rebound.

But Felicity wasn't the phoenix type. Once burnt, she remained ashy. Even after the wedding she had kept clutching that little green trowel that had once belonged to her fiancé, Josh (he was always trying to grow things in their windowbox). Lillian had taken it away from her. Buried it somewhere in the old flat. Along, she hoped, with the grief.

Lillian squelched up the stairs and rang the bell. Felicity and Robert were the first couple to buy one of these Holland Park houses, run so terribly to seed after the war. Well, the first couple anyone knew.

In the sitting room, Robert glanced at her stockinged feet, caked in London mud, and laughed. A rare moment of impishness. Usually, he was so weary, his stomach caved in like a man just gelded. God knows what went on at his surgery. It was in the tough end of Ladbroke Grove. She had always had an urge to smooth his brow. Perhaps that was why it was Felicity he had courted and not her. He always had to be the giver. But Lillian had once been the drowned rat, weeping in St Paul's, with nowhere to go. Until Felicity rescued her.

When they were all seated, Lillian turned to the man on her right, a well-known bookshop tycoon and publisher. She had heard that he was unhappily married to a frigid woman.

'Don't you love this early asparagus? I can't remember eating it in Sydney.'

'My wife has just left me,' replied Angus, calmly, sucking.

'Oh, I *am* sorry,' she said in a thrilled whisper.

'I'm glad. Glad the ice maiden has departed.' He had a nimbleness as he reached for the sauce, young for a businessman. Despite his success, he had accumulated none of the gristle of the boardroom. His enemies called him wily.

He studied her avid, hazel gaze. 'Look, you're not going to go round gossiping are you? I can't stand gossips.'

'I promise,' And to seal the vow she took off her amber necklace and dropped it on the table with a clink.

No one was surprised when they slid off together.

Angus offered Lillian a job in his Oxford Street bookshop, and she became one of his underlings and allies.

'Katherine Feldmann is my best up-and-coming author,' he'd informed her. 'That caustic tone. Every sentence has a sting in the tail. Her short stories are going to be classics. It'll bring back the fashion for short stories. But she doesn't know that yet. She's married to Lucan Feldmann, the archaeologist. He's away in Turkey toiling over a dig in the central Anatolian plains. I think he goes to these remote places so he can escape from the women who besiege him.'

Sometimes Angus would come downstairs from his office and catch her alone in the poetry section and read out aloud to her with his clipped emphasis excerpts from Katherine Feldmann's manuscripts. And sometimes he would say to her magnanimously: 'Why don't you write something for me? You never know. You might have talent.' And she'd reply, not daring to tell him about her attempts at romantic fiction: 'Not me. Everyone's writing for you. I shall retain the elegance of silence.' And he'd laugh gratefully.

The party was still at the muted stage and looked as if it might stay that way. Men in their dark suits juggled politeness with ambition, moving crabwise towards the contacts who might be advantageous, via hangers-on and the upwardly mobile and, most obstructive of all, the wives.

Angus was celebrating his new publishing extension on top of the bookshop. But his greatest coup had been introducing a basement section for poetry, anarchism and radical politics, with lots of browsing chairs and tables and a coffee machine; an idea he had copied from Italy. In the softening climate of the early sixties, all this was magnificent timing. Angus, like Hermes, had the whizzing gift.

Lillian was swirling the whisky around in her glass, a substitute for the sun on this bleak English evening.

'I can quite see why Robert is so partial to this stuff. But how can he booze so much and then get to the surgery every morning, on time?'

'He always does. Wonderful man.' Felicity was eyeing her husband as he approached the bar with the soft, joyous tread of a bridegroom. But she didn't speak of him with the same focused concentration she had once spoken of her fiancé, Josh.

That had been kidstuff, when they were flat-mates in World's End. The scruffy kid from Sydney. And the pale, fragile Felicity from the Home Counties, still bluish under the eyes.

Lillian had always attracted the boys with the sense of drama, prone to cloaks, invariably poets or Poles or anarchists; beating their breasts, predicting early deaths for themselves; swaying dramatically on tops of bridges if she wouldn't relent, then turning to her at midnight with a lustful cry.

Felicity gave little appalled laughs at her remembered antics. She was a one-man woman. And had been engaged at the time to her lovely banker, Josh. He had crinkly hair and played tennis on Saturdays. Felicity played too, her pleated skirt flying; legs thin, slightly bandy, adorable. But then Josh had gone off to the bank's branch in Nigeria and had never written, not once.

Lillian was gazing at a guest by the French windows. Just blew in from Mars. With all the momentum of his flight still radiating from his flesh.

'Grow up, Lil. He's got a huge fan club. He's that famous archaeologist. Married to the writer. Hands off.'

Easier said than done. He had caught her eye and laughed, already in conspiracy.

A brunette was engaging him in conversation, almost on her knees. The trouble with men like that, you have to scrape off other women with a barnacle knife. But he had chosen to wear that red-and-white checked shirt, deliberately provocative, among all the grey suits.

With an effort, she turned back to her best friend. 'Is his wife here. Katherine um . . . ?'

42

'Feldmann . . . Upstairs I think. She had a migraine, so your Angus, and, may I remind you, Lillian, the *host* of this party, took her upstairs to rest.' She waved her hand up and down in front of Lillian's face to cut the lustful beam the incorrigible Lillian was sending out.

'Remember him – Angus. A.N.G.U.S. And you like him. A lot.'

'Like. Yes.'

'Don't mock that word. You can build things on like. Like doesn't let you down. Doesn't change in adversity. I like like.'

Lillian smiled, thinking, Well, she has to, hasn't she?

Felicity's husband was a good citizen, even saintly. A practised saint who was also modest, easily embarrassed, running to fat. A doctor who felt for his patients, who worked on the seamy side of town, where suffering was more obvious and had no end to it.

After Josh had defected, Felicity had consulted him about her depression. He had hoped to cure her with marriage.

Robert was sitting down now, cradling his drink, unattractively sagging. Utterly exhausted from a week's work, he braced himself with booze. Once he must have been good-looking. The birth-mark over his eye might have seemed dashing, like a duelling-scar. Now his shoulders sank, bottle-shaped.

Angus was upstairs with Katherine Feldmann, tucking her in, giving her aspirin, nurturing his best new talent. How he revelled in the role.

Lillian could allow herself to be attracted to Lucan as long as she had not met Katherine. Once, having gazed upon the Medusa head of wives, her desire for their husbands turned to stone. In this, she realized, she was curiously old fashioned. Nice, even.

She smiled brazenly at Lucan Feldmann. He would scoop her up and carry her up the steps of Tara, while one of her satin slippers fell off, disregarded. He would approach her bower, his bronzed feet in silver boots, parting the fronds, covering her with white roses. He would capture her in the Mexican hills and bring her back to his cave, where he would slowly anoint her with subtle oils.

'How are the babies?' she inquired.

'Oh. Cain tried to murder Abel with a poker the other day. A near miss. Robert says it happens all the time, in his practice.'

Grow up, Felicity had said. But what did growing up or liking have to do with the trembling that was starting in the corners of her mouth.

At any moment Mrs Feldmann would enter to claim him, to receive accolades from her fans and rival publishers who wished to sign her up. At any moment Angus, with his shrewd gaze and springy tread, would pop up. 'Hi kiddo? These assholes treating you right?' He would expect her to stay the night afterwards. They would make affectionate love and listen to Charlie Parker, and he would talk tough; dubious trophies from his visits to the States.

But she was rescued from all this ordinariness by the wind. It blew in a sudden gust, opening the French windows; a huge white loop of curtain billowed inwards like a wing, knocking over some wine. The brunette unglued herself from Lucan's feet and raced off to the kitchen searching for salt to put on the wine stains. Lucan looked across to her and laughed. His teeth shone.

Swiftly as a zoom-lens, he came into close-up. His features were large and even but seemed to waver under her stare. His dark hair had a thickness that was not quite English. Celtic perhaps. It churned darkly, but settled when someone closed the window. In the fuss he had remained implacable; had made no move to close it, to be polite. He had not missed her dramatic arrival at his side.

'You're the only free-looking person here,' he said, describing himself.

She was wearing a dark red chiffon dress and jade beads, a present from Angus. But she knew Angus gave richer girlfriends rubies.

'Why have you taken off your shoes?' he said.

They both looked in silence at her large Australian feet, scarred a bit, from corns. 'My shoes hurt. Shoes always hurt me.'

He touched her arm. 'You've got extraordinarily soft skin.' And she was done for. Lava poured over her body. She could feel her nipples rise; a bitch on heat.

The French windows led out directly to the Heath. The shrubs and hedges rattled against the glass. It was a cloudy night in which shadows of clouds ran nervously over the Heath, like rabbits.

'Let's go for a walk on the Heath.'

She made a huge effort. She was a conventional girl. And not unkind. 'Angus would be rather put out. And I believe your wife is upstairs, not very well.'

She turned away from him with pain and watched Felicity, so pale, so frumpish now. Where was her face? Would it emit some clue? But Felicity was bending over the chair trying to wake her snoozing husband.

'Don't worry, the ever-solicitous host has driven his favourite author home. The coast is clear,' said Lucan.

She knew nothing about this man, except that he appeared on TV sometimes, on archaeological programmes. If only Felicity had been close. She would have helped. Felicity, so much the opposite of herself, was like a talisman.

But Lucan was unlatching the window. He had her by the hand, and they sped out into the damp night air to the sound of breaking glass.

The ground was prickly and wet underfoot. The moon kept vanishing, then making dazzling returns. They came to a puddle and she splashed into it.

'Let's hope there isn't going to be another rainfall,' she said brightly.

'Sssssshhh.' With all the necessary firmness, he led her down between the trees where a pond glinted and a lone dog hurried after them.

They came to a tree with overhanging branches, and he lifted the curtain of lime green willow shoots, holding her by the upper arm as if she might escape. Her arm was a Naiad's. Her arm was liquid fire as if she'd been through space.

He put the coat down and pulled her down with him. It was a dance. The great tournament. Breathing fire in a muddy ditch. Delighted by the self as it uncoils. The world became the pinpoint pleasures of breast; two haunches, notched for mating like buck and hind. Eating mud, 'good clean dirt'. Even now she could hear her mother's voice. But she changed its tune; made her approve. 'It's the only vice that's healthy, if you don't force it.' It didn't feel like a sin. The dog joined in, barking, thinking it was a game or a struggle.

At last they were still; the stray rested with its wet muzzle on their muddy legs. 'The Aborigines call a night as cold as this a three-dog night.'

'Sssssshhh. No chat. Don't let's try to civilize it.'

SEVEN

Sonia also worked for Angus, but in a more exalted capacity than Lillian. She shared an office with two other sales reps whom she lulled into a state of chronic whimsy. Her Circean charms, her throaty voice, had them all behaving gallantly and talking elliptically. Whenever she entered the room, they swayed towards her, as if an evening breeze had suddenly swept over a field of wheat.

Sonia wore voluminous, draped clothes which disguised her Central European fatness. But her fatness kept her face unlined, although she must have been in her late thirties. She was of Polish Jewish origin and had had to hide out in a European village during the war as a tiny child, pretending on pain of death to be not Jewish.

Pretending came easily to Sonia. She was trained in guile. Her first husband left her for a woman who never struck attitudes. Sonia was so incensed she ordered twelve dozen red roses to be sent to her rival and billed them to her husband.

'Sonia is marvellous at PR,' Angus confided to Lillian. 'But you have to keep adjusting the footlights all the time.'

Recently, when Angus took Sonia out to a business lunch on the other side of Grosvenor Square, she had crouched down and plucked some grass and shoved it in an envelope. She was going to post it to her latest lover. 'What an operator you are,' Angus marvelled.

Two days after his party, Sonia made a rare descent to the bookshop, and closed in on Lillian. The air rippled around her as if she'd used oars. She was wearing a blouse of some soft petunia colour and a dark, full skirt. Erotic success emanated from every hair on her head.

'I hear you met Lucan Feldmann at Angus's literary soirée?'

Lillian dropped her eyes and stared at Sonia's shoes thinking, She must fly to Milan for them. Her feet and legs in black fishnet; very exotic after the mysterious bulk of her body.

'Did you have a good time?' coaxed Sonia.

'Oh. All the usual crowd. Old faithfuls like Felicity and Robert. The poetry mafia. You know. Why didn't *you* come?'

'Did you talk much to Lucan? He's just come back from a dig on the Central Anatolian plains, has some exciting new theories.'

'No, not much.' Lillian was still young enough to blush. She picked up a pile of novels and marched back into the stock room.

Lillian had been waiting for the telephone to ring. Her face was concrete. She moaned up at the garlands moulded on the ceiling. Then went round to Felicity's to have a cry, to talk about love's famous stomach ache. Felicity knew what it was to have a broken heart.

48

At the bottom of the area steps, nearly kicking over a cloudy milk bottle, Lillian paused and peered into the kitchen. Someone had got there before her. It was Sonia, sitting in untypical naturalness, at her ease; a new rather surprising confidante for Felicity. Lillian felt a prick of jealousy.

She was saying, twisting a strand of hair like a worry bead, turning it greasy, neglecting, for the moment, her appearance, 'God, Felicity, you're lucky you had sons. I was the only daughter. There was just mother and me.' Her throaty voice was reedy with horror. 'That's all there ever were. Mother and me. For all those years. All those meals. Always, just us. No man. No males. No proper family set-up. Ever. Going from room to room.' The keening voice carried out to where Lillian listened.

Felicity stopped, spoon in mid air and glanced at Sonia about to say something. The baby, who sensed he was the stronger, made a grab at her pearls. She had forgotten to take them off and now they gleamed incongruously with her apron and the two safety pins clipped to the strings.

'It was grim, so bleak, all that menstrual tension filling the house. And the only visitors other desperate women.'

Felicity knew that Sonia was touching on her most serious fears. It must be such a strain, thought Felicity, being 'on stage' continually; all that husky, oracular bullshit and all that crossing and re-crossing of legs while the exquisite profile is turned at just the right angle to the light. Felicity felt a sort of pity for her, for all her efforts and the double effort of concealing the effort.

'You can initiate my boys when they're adolescent. You'll make the perfect Older Woman.'

They were chuckling when Lillian let herself in.

She looked distraught. As if she had a wound that needed stitching. 'Robert's upstairs locked in with his paintings.'

'It's you I came to see, Felicity.'

Sonia did not get up to go. But settled back deeper in her

chair, her eyes still, gauging her potential as a rival. Lillian, who had smelt enmity from her at the bookshop, was too silly, too far gone to take heed of discretion. She repeated, 'I simply had to come.'

'Well, Sonia has made one of her rare visits, too.' Felicity had been surprised by Sonia's phone call, her request to see her and the strange interest she had taken in Lillian. Now she could see for herself.

The sound of pearls scattering on the tiles was followed by a howl as Felicity clutched at her throat. 'Christ! My good pearls. Quick!'

She put the baby in the high chair, shoving its teething-ring at it, and the three women crouched on the floor collecting the skidding pearls. In the camaraderie, Lillian forgot the smell of enmity and, when they were all seated around a saucer full of the precious pearls, she blurted out, 'I'm in love!'

Felicity groaned.

'No, really, Felicity.'

'You said that about Derek and Tony and Charles and . . .'

'But none of them made me feel like this. I feel serious for the first time in my life.'

Sonia was instantly sleek with a new assurance. This Lillian played very bad chess.

'It's Lucan Feldmann,' Lillian continued.

'He's married, Lillian,' Felicity said tiredly, glancing away at the garden. She felt anaemic, like her neat lawn and the snapdragons shining greyly under the waning moon.

'I know. I know,' Lillian groaned. 'But you see she wasn't there. She had migraine. She's always getting them. He just scooped me off into the night. The force was magnetic.'

'Women always say that to excuse their home-wrecking,' said Felicity, staring at the complacent Sonia.

Lillian got up and swirled over to the piano, brushing some fallen rose petals from the keys. Felicity had bought the piano hoping that one of her children would be musical; that one day the house would be full of the sound of scales and youthful endeavour. Lillian struck a few dramatic chords in joke-histrionics, but she couldn't keep it up. 'He hasn't rung me!' she cried and put her head on the keys.

Through her sobs she heard a door close. It was Sonia stalking out into the garden in a fit of repulsion, followed closely by the cat, her familiar already.

Lillian felt a hand stroke her head, remembering how Felicity used to comb all the knots out at the back. 'Look darling,' Felicity said, 'the man is married, leave him be. You're just lonely. The most dangerous and erroneous song in the universe is "Someday My Prince Will Come", because he never does. Marry someone like Angus. Someone nice.'

'Oh, there's nothing profound there. Oh ... Felicity.'

Felicity hugged her, and Lillian cried until she looked ugly, except for her eyes which shone like pond-ferns.

The baby cooed, reached a hand out, oddly calmed by this spectacle.

When Sonia came back, she was holding magnolias. They might have been sceptre and orb. Their phosphorescence was part of her own majestic power. She looked with repugnance at Lillian.

Peering up, pushing aside damp hair, Lillian saw this and cringed.

51

EIGHT

Angus slipped upstairs to make a private phone call. Probably to the new girlfriend, the one so rich and careless she left cars unlocked, forgot to take her rings off in the bathroom. Now the drain was blocked.

He expected her to clear up, before the matter-of-fact business of going to bed with him. Upstairs his bed was enormous, heart-shaped. A bit of tycoon trash from LA. Except she couldn't go to bed with him.

She ate the scraps from the bottom of the salad bowl, always the most delicious bits. She blew out the candles and braced herself for the task of telling him she was leaving. She was in a funny mood. She picked up the phone to ring for a taxi. But heard voices still on the line. Lucan's voice.

' . . . driving around at four in the morning, just round and round the city. I'm getting quite acquainted with the dawn. I know what stars go out first.'

'It's that bad, eh?' Angus's lighter tones.

'I just can't get that woman out of my mind. She's like a perfume, she follows you around.'

Bliss is a word with a wing-spread. She knew it. She knew it. It explained his long silence lately. While she had been walking down the street groaning, frightening the pedestrians, he had been wrestling with his conscience.

'Christ, Lucan! Be careful, she's . . .'

Lillian looked at the room, so grand, so chic; no terrorist could demolish it as she could.

'She's a goddess. She's not a doormat.'

'But she's been out to get you for a very long time. Enjoy it, but know you're in the Coils of a Circe . . .'

'People suspect her because she's too beautiful. And her Mata Hari accent makes them think she's phoney. It's her Polishness.'

The eavesdropper, sweating, nearly let the receiver slip out of her hand.

'What's that? Is someone listening?'

'Don't be paranoid. I've got a girlfriend downstairs, but she's too hockey-sticks to do that sort of thing. You know her. The Australian who works in the shop. Lillian.'

'A bit loud.'

'They all are. I'm teaching her to dress.'

'But you understand now why Katherine hasn't delivered the manuscript. She's locked in her room. She won't give me any rope. She won't let me get it out of my system.'

'You and Katherine are an institution. Don't blow it. You'd never get any work done with Sonia.' Nor would Katherine, if he left her, the publisher realized.

Whatever had happened to him on the Central Anatolian plain?

When Angus came downstairs she told him. 'I eavesdropped. I meant to call a taxi, but I couldn't stop listening . . .'

'Poor motherfucker. I suppose you knew already? Everybody does.'

'Even his wife?' She was opening and closing the lid of an enamel box; so Lucan had a full plate.

'She will. But if she ignores it, it'll run its course. And that's why I didn't invite Sonia to the party. But she understood.'

Angus was so urbane. She'd like to throw all his books in their shiny dust-jackets at his clever head.

Angus hadn't noticed or cared, or, if he had, he hadn't said anything. And when she and Lucan had been running to the muddy ditch under that mad moon, it had been Sonia, the uninvited guest, who had been exerting the real magnetic pull.

NINE

Angus sat up to drain what was left of his coffee. He was irritated to see that Lillian had put her mug on top of one of his new books which would undoubtedly leave a coffee-ring stain on the cover. 'Katherine Feldmann's career is taking off. The BBC want her to read her stuff on the Third. She's in demand. All she needs is a good secretary and some home help.'

He turned, the blanket falling off his chest, which he quickly grabbed and held up for warmth. 'How about taking the job, Lillian? You can type well. And housework isn't beyond you. You must be fed up with selling books.'

'Hmmmm.' She equivocated, to hide her disappointment. She had always hoped Angus would promote her; offer her a job as a reader. He knew she could do that sort of thing. But people were always importuning him for work.

'Well, how about it, kid?' He was tickling her back now, between the shoulder-blades, the way she liked.

If she worked for Katherine Feldmann she would feel . . .

uncomfortable, unable to escape the suspicion that she had, well, *sinned*.

'You *are* interested in this job, aren't you? You'd be doing everybody a favour, including yourself. You'd have somewhere much nicer to live. And you'd meet lots of people. She's a celebrity.'

He held her temples with both hands and turned her head so he could peer into her eyes. She closed her eyes hastily, and he laughed and let her go. All the little crustaceans at the bottom of the stones scuttled back in the darkness. They could never meet, her and Angus, soul to soul.

'Of *course* I'm interested.' But she could just imagine Katherine Feldmann's new rented apartment. The furniture shamming dead, the curtains bulging slightly. Her sorrow sticking to the walls; enough to make dogs howl.

She would go to sleep hugging a pillow, thinking of her husband with Sonia, coiled together like twin serpents ... body slaves ... soul mates.

'I overheard Lucan and Sonia laughing away together in the shop last week,' she said in a bitter voice. 'Not at all like partners in crime. She was wearing that petunia blouse, and I overheard her say, "Lillian works here somewhere so beware. One of your endless little acolytes, darling. She writes dreadful poetry, you know. I bet there're reams about you!"'

'Angus's forehead was enormously high, with one prominent vein that throbbed when he was tired. Or perhaps it was simply that his gingerish hair was already receding. 'That woman is *evil*,' he said with sudden, loyal passion.

She was invited, as a matter of course, to Felicity's next dinner party. Stepping into the living-room, recognizing the cushion she'd given them one Christmas, the walls buckled.

'You know Lucan, don't you?'

'Yes. Yes.' In the biblical sense. His face, no longer wavering in ecstatic close-up, had reassembled.

She turned, held out a clammy hand to other guests; saw Sonia sitting by the window, waved in a silly, awkward movement.

How her arms froze, her scalp tingled.

She did not notice the Frenchman until they were seated next to each other, he courteously asking her questions, strangely undrawn by Sonia's beauty. But perhaps, being French, he could see that Sonia was acting.

Lillian could not, at first, hear his words, but became absorbed in the way that he opened his mouth to accommodate one small forkful of food, no more.

He seemed to be discussing Vietnam. Since waking early one morning, staring at the blind, Lillian had made a decision not to worry about Vietnam. She would do their living for them; the dead; the burnt babies. Just as soon as she got over the pain. There are worse pains, more important pains, she knew, than rejection. But most people seemed to be more afraid of it than of atom bombs or famine. More determined to avoid it at all costs.

It must be worse to be Mrs Feldmann.

'You're lucky, living in Paris.' She liked the chiselled, small bones in his face. It took centuries of French civilization to form a face like that. *Bernard.* It sounded nice in French.

'Come over and see me. I'll show you around.' He was scribbling down his name and address, wasting his time. Couldn't he see she had a spear in her side.

'I'm always looking for opportunities to live in Paris,' she said, with peculiar intensity. He was slowly plucking off the leaves of the artichoke, sucking each one slowly. Now he was parting the hair around the centre. Somewhere, on the other side of the table, Lucan and Sonia were pressing feet.

'Leave it to me.' Lillian spread out her good left hand, the one with the long fingers and the pretty ring. Be philosophical in adversity, her mother used to say, clipping the grass, and raking up the jacaranda petals.

'Where did you get this lamb? It's delicious,' said Lillian. Felicity signalled her appreciation of the effort Lillian was making.

'Oh, the butcher gave it to me. His best leg.' Felicity rubbed her forearm distractedly. The dinner parties were her own moral therapy. She hated them. She wanted to lie forever in the foetal position in a darkened room eating chocolates, thinking of Josh.

'*Gives* them to you. What's your secret, darling?' said Sonia, so husky and flirtatious.

'It's Robert. Good old Robert.' Robert looked bashful. 'He gives insulin to the butcher to send to his sister in Bulgaria. This is his thankyou present. So eat up.'

'Tell us what you're working on, Lucan?' Robert wiped a stain from his tie. 'Have you been discovering new civilizations for us?'

'Maybe an ancient religion. The old Earth Mother myth, perhaps?' Lucan admired Robert and would answer his question seriously.

'Oh, Robert's always doing things like that,' interrupted Lillian, still addressing the table with vehemence. 'Do you remember driving me home once when your number plate fell off? The garage owner wouldn't let you pay for fixing it because he told me you'd once come to see his son at two in the morning when he fell downstairs.'

Robert scraped his chair back. An essentially secretive person, this kind of accolade sickened him. Lillian was crass. Felicity was too loyal. He shuffled off to get more wine, his paunch showing through his shirt.

'I come over to London about once a fortnight and buy secondhand furniture and stuff,' Bernard said to Lillian. 'Then every month I ship the lot to my warehouse just near Paris.'

'Am I supposed to commiserate or congratulate?'

'You've picked up my ambivalence about the job. Sometimes I long to be at the Sorbonne, doing a post-graduate course in history and law.'

'But you can't give up the thrill of making money?'

He laughed. She always had grace when she wasn't trying to attract.

'Come to Paris. I'll buy you a meal at La Coupole. Afterwards we will go and sit on Baudelaire's grave. He's buried in the same tomb as his hated father-in-law.'

'Wouldn't it muck up your neat suit?'

The flirting gave her the confidence to look properly at Lucan, and later, after many drinks, she trapped him in a corner. 'You seem awfully happy now. Sonia's slave.'

'Now, now . . . '

'I just want you to realize something.' Lillian spoke with drunken intensity. 'I know you think Sonia is marvellous, worth all the turmoil. She's good for the sprint maybe. But I'm a bloody long-distance runner. You must see that.' He patted her bottom.

Over by the sideboard, Sonia was charming the hostess. Let Lillian make sheep's eyes at Lucan. She would never feel threatened by her again, what with her knobbly hands and split nails as if she laboured in vineyards, her dress rucked-up and stained with wine.

She admired her own hands, their crimson nails bent inwards, as she placed one on Felicity's arm. 'We must lunch.' She was surprised at the thinness of Felicity's arm under the wide sleeve. 'We could go to the Tate.' She had overheard someone say that she had no women friends. Felicity, drab and dutiful. She would do. 'You know, you really should forget the children sometimes.'

Felicity, gratified by this attention, reached to the back of her neck and started rubbing. Her neck was always sore there; near the top vertebrae.

'Poor Lucan has to travel all the time,' said Sonia. 'And when he is back here he is pestered by Katherine in the middle of the night, with some excuse or another. She rings up and asks him to come over and mend the fuse.' She rolled her eyes ceiling-wards. Her thick lashes fluttered. She adjusted her mouth until it achieved the right balance of allure and contempt. 'I think I know the fuse she wanted mending.' She danced a little caper on Katherine's grave.

'I'd love an afternoon at the Tate.'

TEN

It was a freezing spring day in London. Bus drivers stopped too long at bus stops in order to miss the lights at the next intersection. The faces of gentle mini drivers took on a hawkish, killer impatience.

Despite the introspective weather, few people had wandered into Angus's bookshop for a browse. Lillian crouched down to dust the coffee-table tomes. Their prices had been slashed several times, but customers still remained unenticed by their contents.

Angus popped his sandy head around a pile of nineteenth-century poets. She looked alert, hoping for a dinner at Wheelers or a night out. She was still one of his favourites, after all. 'Lillian, I forgot to give you Katherine Feldmann's number.'

A living poet slid up behind Angus, his small eyes hooded to hide their untrustworthy plots. 'Poor old Katherine. She must be suffering?' he probed. 'Still it was only a matter of time.'

Angus scribbled down the telephone number.

'It was inevitable that Katherine would unload him,' the poet persisted.

'It wasn't like that,' said Angus irritably. 'He got the *coup de foudre*, poor bastard. Thunder and lightning.'

'For Sonia? Who hasn't? In their time? She and Lucan have met each other's match. All his other things were just peccadilloes.'

Lillian felt depressed. All the books depressed her. Egos jostling for position. Poets were the most malicious people on earth. Perhaps she would ring Katherine Feldmann about that job.

At her flat in World's End the hammering went on and on. She had kept it on after Felicity had married. But now the decorators were working on the hall. They had painted the walls white, and the old cracked brown linoleum was spotted with white paint. But it would be ripped up soon and something modern would be put down. They would install double-locks and an intercom system. It was inevitable the rent would go up. She would have to move. The job as secretary to Katherine Feldmann seemed more viable every minute, and at least she would be able to write her own stories. She would write about love, of course, and betrayal.

She lay down on her bed, staring up at a sparrow's droppings on the glass of the skylight. If only she could sleep. She never had enough sleep.

The janitor with the glass eye disturbed her, handing her a postcard with immense reluctance as if he was doing her a favour. It was from Paris, from Bernard, 'How about that dinner at La Coupole?' was all it said.

She tossed it on the mantelpiece. Tight-arsed little frog.

After an endless winter, the sun shone feebly and people inhaled the air with wonder as if it was rare old brandy.

The garden at the back of the Marsh house was full of white petunias. Felicity tried to return a stray ladybird to a blade of grass, but it kept crawling back up her hand. Ladybirds always made her feel lucky.

She scooped it away with the edge of a sticky leaf, then lay back exhausted in a deep deck chair. The contraceptive hadn't worked; or she had put it in the wrong way, sliding it over the cervix which, in her case, lay flat against the back of her insides.

Robert was supposed to have taken this Saturday off, but the publican's son had come down with mumps. Felicity hoped alcoholism was not hereditary. At least Robert was pleasant.

She felt great fondness for him, but there had never been any spark. Not like with Josh. And yet there had been no problem creating life. It didn't follow, she supposed. Sometimes looking at her children when they slept, she was sorry for them. Perhaps they would lack the essential spark.

But what she had done, marrying Robert on the rebound, was better than drifting, like poor Lillian, hoping for something that never happened.

At that thought, the baby kicked. It was just a tiny flutter, a butterfly's wing, but the first one and, despite herself, tears sprang to Felicity's eyes. It was the one absolute miracle. No wonder the ancients had built a shrine for the giving of birth. It seemed far more appropriate than a hospital.

Robert had suggested an abortion, but she couldn't face it. No. No. No. In her mind she saw a coffin. A grave.

She had been walking through an old disused cemetery recently and had stood by a grave with no headstone and felt unbearably sad. It was as if her insides were falling out; entrails tumbling to the ground. That grave was for the baby she never had with Josh. Or was it for Josh himself? In the twentieth century you weren't supposed to pine away and die. You were supposed to get over things. She kept having babies, consciously or unconsciously, to populate a hollow world.

Her two-year-old was lurching about in the buttercups. The eldest kept pretending to hold them under his chin to see if he liked butter and then surreptitiously cramming them into his mouth. Cain poisoning Abel.

With an effort, Felicity bent over and pulled the flowers from their clenched hands. They both let out a wail. How they hated her for that moment.

Behind her on the grass she heard Lillian approaching. She usually dropped in after her Saturday morning shopping. Today she was wearing a skirt that seemed much too short; the hems were crawling up every year.

Lillian plopped down on the grass, reaching over to retrieve a cauliflower that rolled out of the basket.

'Something rather extraordinary has happened.'

'Oh God. Not in love again?'

'No, no. It's just that they've been decorating our old house in World's End and underneath the lino in the hall they've found lots of letters.'

She started to put her vegetables on the lawn.

'And there's one for you. They think that old janitor stuck them there, looking for cash, and then hid them under the lino. Here you are. It's incredibly out of date.'

Felicity took the letter and stared at the Nigerian stamp. Africa, the imponderable. What had happened to Josh in Africa? Lillian laughed at a ladybird and sang the old song:

Your house is on fire
You children are gone

She blew it away, a tiny brown helicopter.

'Aren't you going to read it? You see, he did write, after all that. And you gloomed for ages about that. I couldn't think why. Josh was so dull. Do you remember him plodding over

64

with the trowel and the plants for our windowbox? Aren't these early vegetables lovely? How's the morning sickness? Shall I make you a cuppa while you read it?'

When Lillian returned with the tray, Felicity had the letter back inside the envelope.

She could always count on Lillian to be too self-absorbed to ask questions.

'I'm absolutely fed up with the bookshop,' Lillian's voice came from somewhere in space. 'Do you think I should take on a menial job as dogsbody to Katherine Feldmann? If I worked in someone's house all day, I could knock out some work of my own in my spare time ...'

Felicity sat back, as if to listen, stuffing the yellowing letter up the sleeve of her cardigan, hiding her shock. It was a proposal of marriage from Josh. He did get round to it after all.

ELEVEN

Katherine Feldmann was found dead in her new flat at 10 am on Monday that freezing spring.

The Sunday papers contained a special tribute from many writers and critics. It included the publication of one of her extraordinary last stories, which Angus had not had time to read before her death.

The coroner was told that a neighbour saw Katherine Feldmann put the key under the mat on the night before her death. She had said she was expecting someone to come early the next morning and let herself in.

It looked as if this suicide was a cry for help.

MEETING THE NATIVES

TWELVE

'You don't have to catch the last ferry tonight?'

Lillian hesitates. If she gets a taxi to the Quay now she'll be in good time for the ferry, then home to her lumpy single bed. She can lie with her feet pointing to the waves; the night-sea unfolding. But she'll be too late to listen to the jazz on 'Music to Midnight'.

They are leaving a Sydney cinema. The film has been about lesbians and full of slow, somnambulistic close-ups of one woman gazing at another. Lillian decides that it has bored her. But she is glad to get out of that cinema crammed with hot-eyed women. She feels a borderline repulsion, but fears that this feeling must be reprehensible.

'Oh, all right, I'll go back to your place for coffee. But I have to get in to the paper tomorrow morning.'

'I'll drive you home in an hour or so.' Lillian gets into Terry's car which is full of small mysterious bits of sailing tackle. At her house she hears the voices of the radicals raised in agreement. She by-passes the communal kitchen and heads upstairs.

'Where do you think you're going?'

'I can't face the thought-police right now. Let's have a drink in your room.'

She runs on ahead and finds a spot near the stacked records. Although the house belongs to Terry, she shares it democratically. The others resent her making the slightest reference to the harsh facts of her ownership.

Consequently, Terry has no privacy, except in her bedroom. They select Parcifal. Waves of Wagner crash against the shores of lonely coastlines, mounting and mounting. Lillian tries to concentrate on Terry's poetry.

'It's probably great. But I can't decipher riddles. I'm losing my eyesight, too, a sign of senility.' She gives up. Flops in girlish camaraderie on Terry's big bed. Looks up at the large swaying lampshade. It could hypnotize you. Oddly voluptuous in such a spartan household.

Terry lies next to her and reads *Eloise and Abelard*. Wagner pours forth entreaties. Lillian can't remember when she last lay on a bed with someone. She starts muttering. 'Marriage was so strange. My marriage. I used to say to him, "Listen, sleep somewhere else, downstairs in the library or with your beady-eyed mistress or something. I'm sick of playing tombstones in bed." And the odd thing is that I think he loved me all the time. Still does. Ever since he first asked me to Paris to La Coupole. Once he had to go to his mother's house for something. I waited outside the huge wrought-iron gates at Neuilly, not wanting to get involved with boring French *politesse*. It was dark. I crouched beside a parked car. I wanted to have a pee. It shot off sideways and spattered a shining white Citroen. Bernard came out and was delighted! I had defiled his mother's car. *Quelle anarchiste!* He fell for me then, completely, and proposed. But it's no use. His mother or the Lycee had done their worst. He's just a cold fish. He was trained to be one. Like

68

those vines in the Luxembourg Gardens. I suppose I could have taken lovers for the cinq-a-sept, but I had to run the house around him and the boys and protect him from humiliation and entertain, and anyhow the lovers would have resented being treated like a canape, gobbled up quickly, abstractedly. So I had virtually no love, no truth, no *skin*. All that secrecy. All that wrongness ... I would have got cancer if I'd let it continue. I could almost feel the cells start to turn malignant.'

Terry nods, half listening to the banal tale of a marriage gone wrong, half reading.

The traffic noise outside is now occasional. Pinned on the wall is a postcard reproduction of a Roman soldier. Very male.

'The boys chose to stay with Bernard. They chose sides. At that stage they were in greater need of the male influence. But Bernard is too busy to discipline them. He spends his life in aeroplanes. Fabrice has been kicked out of university. Jerome failed to get in, though, Gods knows, I begged them to study until I was hoarse.'

Last week she had come across an old photograph of herself with both arms around them, on a beach, near Cannes. They had rushed up to her out of the foam, aged eight and ten. She had held her arms out wide to receive the impact of their sandy bodies.

Frangipanis smell sweetest at night. She can smell them as they wing past the windows, falling whitely off the tree outside.

Like a reflexive jerk of a corpse, Lillian's arm mutinies from her long-held rigidity. It reaches over, without rhyme or reason, to the body of the person beside her. It hooks itself over Terry's body. It takes both women by surprise; a submarine risen from the unconscious.

There is silence. Silence. The record has stopped. Terry puts down *Eloise and Abelard* and turns towards Lillian. The book slides off the bed as her body turns, and it lands with a loud thud. Terry says something incomprehensible and kisses her.

She surfaces. 'What did you say?'

'You know. When Eloise and Abelard first kiss: "And then they put away their books."'

Adventure sings in Lillian's ears. She can hear oars rip in the water, as a rudder changes direction. Weirdness and pleasure mix. Lillian springs up and takes off her clothes quickly, embarrassed.

When she was fourteen in bed with her bosom friend, they tickled each other's back, prudishly stopping at the waist.

Now she was about to go down in a diving-bell. 'You're my first lady love and my last, I know,' Lillian announces finally.

But she wants to get away. She kneels down by the bedside and murmurs, 'I'd rather go now. I don't want to face the bean-sprouts in the morning.'

She creeps out of the silent, dark house, wondering which room Terry's son sleeps in. Outside in the dawn light she steps on dropped frangipanis littering the pavement, all negligent glamour, like houris. She picks one up and inhales its yellow centre and stops at a popular Sydney graffiti sprayed on the wall: LAND RIGHTS FOR GAY WHALES.

Laughing, she runs on down the hill in search of a taxi, feeling she's just made a parachute jump.

The early hosing of the nature-strips has left beads of water, bluish on the cropped grass. It's the sweat on Terry's chest. On the ferry she looks at the whole world salaciously; even prim secretaries doing their crochet; even the labourer with a beery face hurling the rope over the bollard. She can see them all as newborn babies, their toes curling, having their tummies tickled, equal recipients of bliss.

But the fever, the novelty, abates. She sits at her desk worrying over the article she is writing on the Ananda Marga.

The editor looks over her shoulder. He puts a heavy hand on her shoulder, making her blood jolt. He's wearing a wedding ring. How conventional. 'The cops are convinced they did the Hilton bombing job.'

She looks up, not meeting his gaze. 'Most people are. They're guilty until proved innocent. They're this weird, foreign-sounding cult, you see. Make perfect scapegoats.'

'Get over to their Newtown offices. Get hold of some of the roneoed newsletters for members only. Read the propaganda. You'll learn how weird they are.'

What she likes about the job, hitting the pavements, playing cops and robbers, is that it keeps you busy.

Going home on the ferry she is pleased she is no longer a danger to the community. She is inhabiting a city in which half the citizens are sexually without threat. Women have slipped back into comfortable neutrality. She can relax in their presence again. Tired women and girls pressing up next to her in the crowd have regained their ordinariness. The men, heads concealed behind the racing news in the evening papers, have temporarily laid down their weapons.

But Terry has taken on a hooded aspect. She is an enigma, not like the others in her devil's kitchen. She does not think in categories or trends. She is too obliquely clever for that game.

She watches the serpent-writhe of water before the prow, allowing the spray to bathe her tired face. Terry could not have touched her first. And as for her, well, it was the exception that proved the rule, she supposed. Perhaps it was to do with being lonely.

THIRTEEN

'Look! Look! Dolphins!' Lillian looks up from the tilting deck where she is crouched, head held low in case the boom wheels. Dozens of dolphins are in mid leap in the foam of an incoming tanker. They hurl themselves skywards, twisting in glistening curves, then slap back into their element. A shiver goes through them both. To see dolphins like this. They must be on a lucky streak.

The tanker moves towards the Harbour, leaving the dolphins to emerge seconds later behind another ship ploughing through the wild.

'Aren't they having fun? They're playing.' Terry's screwed-up eyes meet Lillian's for once.

The shivering mountains of water rise and fall. Lillian has tried to get control by concentrating on the rope drill, but now, having seen the leaping dolphins, she is in God's eye-beam. Fear vanishes.

The women lie together on the bunk with the hatch closed. Lights dapple over the bed like fish's scales. The boat rolls back and forth.

You can see the old dock one second, then the deserted beach.

Lillian is chattering: 'People are always dividing things into things. The four great female archetypes: Diana, Venus, Ceres, Minerva. What does it boil down to: *Diana* – the mystic, the solitary wood-rambler; *Venus* – sexual passion; *Ceres* – the grain goddess, the nurturer, the mother; *Minerva*. Now she is interesting. The most powerful. I think she is sexless. She can make or do. She becomes prime minister. She might become president one day. And we are *all* of these archetypes at different times!'

'We are sometimes sexy, sometimes maternal, sometimes mystic, and sometimes we want to get up and change the world. How original!'

'You're spoiling my fun. I was about to say that we neglect any of these goddesses, we fail to sweep out their temples or place offerings on their altar-steps, at our peril. For some time now, certain groups have been trying to discredit Ceres. The soft, sweet nurturer. But she is about to take a terrible revenge!'

'Oh Christ, spare me a lot of rubbish about the "wise womb". And isn't it about time Minerva had her say at long last?' laughs Terry. 'No, I'll bring on the booze and we can pay serious tribute to a male god, Bacchus.'

'Oh make him Dionysus. He's more interesting.'

'I'll go with your mood then. I'll read you something I just happen to have right here.' Terry roots round under the bunk and finds Katherine Feldmann's *Collected Works*. The twenty-fifth edition.

Lillian stirs. Blankets slide away from her shy, white body, undamaged much by motherhood. 'No, something else. Anything else.'

'But they're marvellous. Just listen to this . . .'

'I do know them. I've heard them all. *Ad nauseam*.'

Terry snaps shut the book, disconcerted.

'I knew her very slightly, in London.'

Terry lights a tiny cigar. She loves yarns. 'Odd wasn't it, her bumping herself off like that? A woman of her potential. Think what she might have still contributed. And didn't she have a child or a husband or something?'

Lillian puts her feet on the tilting floor, thinking of doors closing just when you need them to open. Angus had told her about Katherine's last visit. She had come to his office one evening when he was packing up to go on holidays.

And now all the doors in the universe are open to Katherine Feldmann. Grants. Prizes. Doctorates. Honours.

Lillian scratches her head all over as if to dislodge fleas.

'Look, go and get something else. The *Oxford Book of English Verse*. Read us some John Donne.' But Donne is ineluctably heterosexual.

'I wonder by my troth what thou and I did till we loved?' asks Terry. Donne leaps over Time's battlement like Errol Flynn.

Sea-light ripples with the sway of the boat, scaling their bodies; one suntanned and firm, one soft and white, shy and shimmering with unused eroticism.

The yellow curtains blow apart, revealing more of the cove and headland of Quarantine Bay and beyond that the distant pines of Manly. A cormorant hovers over a foolish fish that swims too near the light. Then swoops.

'Terry I feel so right with you. I just wish you were a man.'

Terry breathes in sharply. 'Do you know what you're saying? Do you understand the significance of what you're saying?'

Lillian blinks. Terry stares at the ashtray. 'That's the trouble with being a lesbian. Women despise each other.'

Returning to Manly at the end of the weekend Lillian sees a pile of what looks like rubbish outside her flat door. There is a plastic dish-rack and various half-used groceries. Ah, Bruiser must have had a big haul on the beach. She brings them inside. But they seem too utilitarian for Bruiser. He usually gives her clothes and once a picture of two love-birds kissing which he said he had found on the sand (although she suspected from his lovelorn look that he had acquired it especially).

'Am I a lesbian?' She is mulling it over when the telephone rings. The first call since it was installed on Friday. She runs to answer it, agog for the outside world. She has been stranded for too long.

'Lillian?'

'Hullo?' She knows who it is. But she waits, making him announce it.

'It's Bernard.'

Her stomach contracts. 'You're the first person to ring me.'

'I rang your family in the mountains and they told me you'd just had it installed. How are you?'

'Fine. I've been away all weekend sailing, outside The Heads!'

'Look, I could come to Australia. There's a lot of good Victoriana out there. It might be worth exporting.'

'Where will you stay?' she says with meaningful precision. 'You can't stay here.'

'You must have a spare room. After all, you could put me up. I need a few days on holiday too. You're lolling around, and you left me to cope with everything. Ever since we moved back to London the boys have run amok.'

Snakes have more venom after they've been lying low; she'd read that somewhere. 'You *know* I invited the boys to join me. But they won't leave their bands and their girls. They're grown up now. Everything they know is over there.'

'So you just walk out to indulge your sentimentality about a country you haven't seen since you were a child.'

'It was that or a nervous breakdown.'

'Perhaps it's the menopause. You women go dotty.'

She hangs up and goes out on the balcony, breathes deeply. I've escaped. I've escaped. She repeats it to herself each time a wave slaps the shore.

In the house next door the lights are on, the windows open. Shirley, her head in a scarf, is sweeping up. She yells, 'Did you get the stuff I left you? Might come in handy.'

'Thanks, Shirley. Where are you off to?'

'He's finally got the money to take us all back to New Zealand. So we're going before the old man turns up.' She pulls a face.

'I'll miss you, Shirley!' Miss you. Miss you. The words echo over the pines where the parrots are doing their evening screech and flutter.

That's the trouble with Manly, people coming and going. Like the birds. The surfer has vanished. Although his surf-board is still on the balcony. He'll probably surface soon.

The sea that night boils and fumes, reacting to the typhoons up north. It lashes all the way down here like the tail of a dragon. The sewage washes back on the each, and the pines lose so many needles Bruiser will need a shovel to clear them up tomorrow.

All through the night the front door bangs and bangs. When she listens to some jazz before sleeping, it sounds as if someone is banging on her floor in rage, but it's probably just another manifestation of the wind. That new tenant with the blue eyes who has moved in below can't possibly object to a quiet bit of music.

These old houses have such ancient plumbing, so many alterations have been done on the cheap. The big rooms with the pressed-tin ceilings have been divided into two. The plumber and mason are constantly being called in to correct faults. And twice since she's been there Lillian has saved the house from burning down. The first time she'd seen a flame licking out of an electric wire on the stairs; and a few weeks later she'd smelt burning from the flat below before the hippies moved out. Both times she had raised the alarm.

Sometimes she thinks the house is held together with pins and will collapse in the next wind storm. It is so near the sea it creaks like a boat. The spray flies in the window. The seagulls shit on it, the wind rocks it, pipes burst in its bowels, and occasionally the lone voyagers go mad.

In the morning the balcony is full of pine needles. Tea towels she'd put out there to dry and bleach have blown away. So have the family next door.

FOURTEEN

Through the wire fence of the Far West Children's Home the kids stand and stare at the liquid blue. Many are Aborigines. Their previous glimpses of water have been of outback dams flashing like broken mirrors, surrounded by birds.

Lillian stands and stares at them in their playground, at the shrinking, stick-like way their bodies move.

She goes on to the library, where an old woman in fancy dress is browsing through romantic novels. She is wearing torn fishnet stockings and a scarlet mini-skirt. Her carmine lipstick spots her remaining yellow tooth.

Lillian begins the search for reference books.

'Brat!'

The scream in the library is followed by a wail.

The old tart has hit the child with a copy of *Love's Springtime*. His mother and the librarian bear down. The dispute begins about who cast the first stone.

Lillian escapes to the esplanade and sits on a beach, hectored by gulls, watching a surfer tumble on the crest of a wave, his board hurtling up in the air, roped to his brown leg. She wonders how often that has to happen before you get to ride the perfect wave.

She leaves the keys of her flat with Merla at the fish shop to be collected by an old school friend, a jazz-singer who has come down from Queensland for a few days.

Tomorrow she is going on holidays with Terry, leaving at dawn. Their destination is Nimbin, the old hippy colony where Terry owns land. Terry has had the car serviced in preparation for the eight hundred kilometre haul to her timber house which she allows friends to use rent-free for doing work on the land.

'You'll love it. It's in the shadow of Mount Warning. Very magical. People are still trying to live that dream. No getting and spending and grabbing. Surviving on as little as possible to conserve the world's resources.'

They go to bed early to get a good sleep before the drive. But in the middle of sleep their bedroom door squeaks open.

Lillian, after a lifetime of motherhood, wakes up at the slightest noise and sees in the grey light, Terry's twelve-year-old son.

Her first instinct is to hide. But she leaps up, wraps a blanket around herself and scuttles towards the door where the boy stands, staring.

She bends down and puts her hands on his shoulders.

'You should knock before you come in,' she whispers. He stares at her with a light in his eye. Curiosity? Lewdness? 'Look,' she is brisk with anguish, 'the only reason I'm here is because your mother is very special to me. She is not like any other woman I have ever met.'

The bedside lamp goes on. She hears Terry's grating laugh.

'Sprung! We've been sprung!' laughs Terry amiably.

'Mum, where's my skateboard?'

'It's in the tool cupboard.' Terry looks carefully at the still floundering Lillian, tripping on the edge of her blanket.

'Okay. Have fun up north.' He leaves, closing the door.

Lillian slumps heavily on the edge of the bed.

'What are you fretting about?'

'I don't believe it.'

'Believe what?'

'All that trendy bullshit about not needing roles. I remember walking along the road when I was little looking up at the men and women and thinking about it and deciding that I was glad there were two sexes. I loved the idea of duality, even then. All creation is built around it, for Christ's sake.'

'Not *all* of nature accords with it.' Terry lit a small cigar.

'Don't start quoting one or two obscure examples of birds or bees or turtles who go for the same sex. I don't think it can be much good for kids to see Dad making love to blokes and Mum with her girlfriend. It must make them feel threatened by chaos.'

'Does my son look as if he's threatened by chaos?'

'He looks remarkably well adjusted.' Lillian is thinking of her own sons. How would they react if they found out? Wouldn't it be another thing that might alienate them? They might wear their freakish haircuts in defiance of the chill that had hung over the household, but they were conventional boys. And she didn't believe that dualism was a bourgeois plot.

'The difference between the sexes is more than conditioning and a lot of soft engineering.'

'That's not going to go down very well with the gay movement now suppurating in my kitchen,' laughs Terry.

'For a start, men have erection anxiety. They have this terrible secret worry about getting it up. They're frightened they'll disappoint the women. That's why they have to be treated with care, poor, delicate creatures.'

'That's conditioning, too. Why should they be so anxious to please?'

'Oh, Christ! Human beings like to please. We don't have anything equivalent to that. We can fake if needs be. It's not so dazzlingly humiliating for us if our body doesn't respond.'

'We can always become lesbians, can't we? If the worst comes to the worst,' says Terry sarcastically.

'But we have another anxiety that men will never understand – our fertility-span is cruelly limited. It's really only at about the age of twenty-five that most women are prepared to think about giving up their freedom and having babies. That gives them fifteen years. Fifteen little years until they're forty to find the right man to start a family with! Men have forever. Women feel washed up, finished, menopausal when they're no longer fertile. That's because men make them feel like that, I know. But it's also because they can't have any more babies, and they know it. And mostly they age quicker. It isn't the same for men. It's quite usual for a fifty-year-old man to have a twenty-five-year-old bride. But I agree with you, that's got to do with money and status.'

'Oh, Gawd.'

'And women aren't so crazy. Can you imagine six hundred thousand of them marching off to Russia to fight at the beginning of winter?'

'Easily. Look come back to bed and stop all those old-fashioned wails.'

'I don't see what's old fashioned about it. It just *is*! You remind me of the old hippies who used to say there was no such thing as jealousy. So they pretended; they shared and shared alike, sexually, and jealousy came out in extremely nasty repressed forms. Ask anyone who's ever lived in a commune!'

'I could argue. I could clobber you with words like "epistemology". But I'll stick to the point. You think the sons of lesbians are automatically doomed?'

81

'Not necessarily. But possibly there will be some ill effects that we can't foresee.'

'So you think the disorder of going against the law of the universe will unhinge them?'

'I don't think it helps matters. Once you're grown up, you can smoke dope until you're blue in the face and have sex with anything that moves. But I think children do grow better (I'm sorry!) in a wholesome, orderly environment, as long as it's warm and affectionate. That sounds boring, I know. Chaos, of any kind, just doesn't help.'

Terry grinds the cigar out. 'It doesn't help to grow up glued to foul TV programmes, or swim in polluted seas. Do you remember all those periwinkles and anemones and sea-horses that used to cling to the rocks when we were kids? All gone now. Killed off. And it doesn't help to have this lousy Liberal government we always vote in after a brief flirtation with the left. We want a stern conservative prick on top, otherwise we feel uneasy. And it doesn't help to have wife-beating and baby-bashing and non-stop wars and drunken, uprooted Aborigines. For Christ's sake, why don't you worry about important things?'

'I can't do anything about those things,' says Lillian, flinging off the blanket, falling into bed, turning her back. 'What life will my worrying save?'

Soon she turns again and lies staring up·at Terry's sensual lamp swaying in the breeze, telling herself how amusing it is to take a conservative line with Terry because all the other anarchists in the house agree with each other. Agree all the bloody time.

They mistake contention for hostility. But this time she was not really just playing mental tennis. Belting down a few bracing serves for Terry to volley back. It had worried her, when Terry's son had come into the bedroom. She had hated it.

During the long drive north, Lillian keeps admiring the fortitude of Terry. For twelve hours she keeps at the wheel, refusing help, her woollen hat pulled low over her determined face.

The north coast of New South Wales unwinds its gum trees, hotels, Holdens, service stations, pizzerias, hamburger joints, and long golden beaches, their coarse sand dented with footprints. 'The more you travel in this goddamn country the more it's the same,' Lillian complains.

Aching with fatigue, they finally quit the car. Fresh air stings in the darkness. Smells of cream and cow-dung and clover. Beasts shuffle in the shed. A stream tinkles somewhere across a sloping paddock.

But the house is semi-derelict. The mattress unsheeted, stained. The windows curtainless. Exhausted, repulsed, Lillian flops asleep, after pushing her suitcase hard against the door of her room.

The holiday did not improve.

'You really don't want to be here, do you?' says Terry in a squashed voice as Lillian lies, later that day, staring at the flaking walls. The damp patches resemble France . . . England . . . America . . .

The caretaker's wife has all the meanness of some fat women, resenting Lillian's presence and showing it by slamming drawers and cupboard doors.

A guru from nearby drops in and bores her with his self-righteous solemnity. He has the temerity to ask them all to sit cross-legged in a circle and chant. When a child in the group mistakes the game for ring o' rosies and jumps in the middle, the guru doesn't even smile.

Lillian ambles down to the river and hangs underwear to dry on a blackberry bush. She closes her eyes and hears the locusts start up like the hum of a refrigerator. She brushes a blowfly off her nose . . .

A lorry-driver, taking the short-cut on the timber route

from Cairns, is startled to see two women sitting sadly on the bridge; the small dark one seems to be pleading with the big redhead in the floral dress.

Round the compost-heap flying insects copulate in mid air. The hostile caretaker is boiling lentils. The record-player doesn't work. They have to eat a lot of pumpkin.

In the local township addicts reel from cafés. Shop-fronts are painted with all the brio of the late sixties. Covered in suns that smile.

But the fantasy-suns are faded by the real sun. Notices pinned to tree trunks advertise meditation centres, psychic massage, astrological acupuncture. This is the most Eastern point of the continent. It picks up Californian pollen.

Lillian finds a phone box that works and rings the Ananda Marga office. 'Okay,' she trills, 'I *will* have dinner with you,' and gives a loud flirtatious chuckle 'but you'll have to tell me more about your organization.'

Circling the phone box Terry has the stricken look of somebody about to be sent away on a long, unfamiliar journey.

There is a valedictory moment. It is so warm it could be mistaken for a honeymoon. They dive into the lake, into the sunset's red reflection. They look at each other. Look and look. Terry is trying to unhinge Lillian's decision to go. Lillian is trying to imprint this moment, for old time's sake.

Lillian is alone again at her front door holding a battered suitcase. The jazz-singer has left the key on top of the ledge. Inside Lillian finds a note on the kitchen table:

'You have a crazy bloke downstairs. He pulled a knife on

me. I'm coming down again in a couple of months. See you then.'

Lillian sits holding the note, waiting for an egg to boil. There is such a thing as being straight, more or less.

WEBS OF COMPROMISE

FIFTEEN

Lillian was walking briskly down Mount Street when she recognized Lucan coming towards her.

He stopped dead. He gazed. He had a hint of an ironical, testing smile. His once glossy hair was streaked with grey. And he had a new hardness of body, as if he'd been on combat duty.

Lillian hesitated. She looked as if she didn't recognize him, put her head on one side and gave a baffled half-smile. And moved on. He had stopped dead as if to say, At last we have our chance.

She walked away from him in the street, pretending she didn't know him. She put it down to fear.

Lillian trailed upstairs and listened outside the nursery door. All, for once, seemed to be well. Felicity's new-born was genial from the start, as if all the anxiety given off from their marriage had been absorbed by the eldest two. She could hear the deep breathing of the middle child; asphyxiated by his bossy older brother; eclipsed by the ravishing new arrival. Felicity had asked her to be godmother to the firstborn, but that unlucky second was her favourite.

The door of Robert's studio was ajar. She peeped in, attracted by smells of linseed and paint. Robert didn't like to show people his paintings. He was reticent about all the things that mattered to him. He wouldn't talk about his patients, and he wouldn't talk about his paintings.

There was one canvas that looked particularly morbid, although they all seemed somewhat murky. Over by the wall, stacked on top of a lot of other canvasses, was a picture of Felicity as a madonna. Her head was a skull and all the babies she so tenderly brooded on were little skulls.

Lillian shuddered. Painting, she told herself, was a healthy outlet. She heard a car drive up and the cheerful noises of goodnight. She ran downstairs intending to fling open the door, but paused.

Through the curtain crack she saw Sonia enthroned in the driver's seat. Where was Lucan? Sonia was sitting close beside Felicity. Bosom pals. The rose and the leaf that sets off the rose.

Robert struggled up the front step and tinkered about with the keyhole, missing every time. Perhaps he was like that in bed. No one took his alcoholism seriously, even though he'd lost his licence; he always remained so amiable.

'Come in for a coffee, Sonia,' Felicity entreated, out of the car now. 'Say hullo to Lillian. She's babysitting.'

'No, darling. I'm exhausted. But remember what I said,' Sonia intoned in her stagey contralto: 'Don't fret. Remember, it's fate.'

The three children slept deeply, riding their leviathan dreams.

The middle boy, as usual, had his leg stuck out of the blanket as if ready to sprint. For some time their mother gazed upon them, her shirt stained purple with wine.

She had never had post-natal depression. Far from it. It had been post-natal ecstasy for her. Partly, it was relief, that the offspring was not deformed. But the feeling was too profound to be only that. It lasted too long.

But it was not the sea-bed she had touched with Josh. She should have had more faith. A compromise marriage, even to a nice guy, was debilitating.

Each object in Angus's apartment shone from the attentions of his char lady, over whom he kept a vigilant eye.

Lillian had been asked to the party in the unvolatile capacity of ex-girlfriend. But there was something brittle in the air.

'I'll need a new reader, Lillian. You'd like that, wouldn't you? You could work upstairs, near me.' He loved to fix things. A form of generosity, or power-play.

'No, Angus. I'm going to have a crack at Paris.'

She enjoyed her detachment. It was her way of punishing him. He had dived in, but he had not swum across the lake. He had not taken her seriously.

When the guests were on their second drinks, Angus instructed them to treasure their first editions of Katherine Feldmann's *Collected Works*. 'They'll be collectors' items. You'll see.' It was if he'd blown a whistle. The gossip started up all over the room.

'Do you remember what big feet Katherine had? Size ten. Somehow one doesn't imagine Emily Brontë or Jane Austen with big feet.'

'My ex fancied her. He always said women who looked like that were all sexpots underneath. He was going to make a pass at her. But never got round to it.'

'Engrave that on his headstone.'

'She rang me up. I said I'd ring back. But I fell asleep. I'd been overdoing it. She killed herself the next morning! I wonder how many people she rang that day were unavailable?'

'I went round to her new flat, but just once. I couldn't wait to get out. The atmosphere was . . . it smelt of dejection.'

'Rejection, probably.'

'She must have felt like a pariah. She had always been such a success. Failure embarrassed her.'

'He left her for the greatest blow-job on earth.'

'Shut up, for God's sake,' Angus ordered.

'You're like crows on a ploughed field. And that's Lucan at the door now. He's had the subject, up to here.'

He looked like a Roman soldier, glorious, still, but haunted by battlefields. To speak to him was an effort. People had to take deep breaths, adjust their faces before embarking on it.

He slumped in the chair, battle-weary, unshielded. Lillian resisted an impulse to unlace his shoes, wash his feet in her hair. She closed the file on that younger her with a decisive snap.

In a corner she found that same malicious poet. Still up to his old tricks.

'Lost his beauty hasn't he? Guilt, I suppose.'

'You'd never suffer from such a thing, would you?'

'I don't believe in guilt?'

'You amaze me. I always know what the next fashion is going to be by talking to you.' She smiled at him. 'Anyhow, I'm sure you believe in envy.'

When Lucan moved to stub out a cigarette, he had to move carefully. Not that he was awkward. Just big-boned. But there was something more wooden than magisterial about his silence tonight. Angus, who could slip in and out of Hell with agility, approached him cosily.

'Liked your programme on Central Anatolia. Those bulls-heads on the wall did look like uteruses and fallopian tubes, once you'd pointed it out.'

'Well, the bulls-heads have no eyes. That's the clue. And they're in the most holy temple where the birth chair was found. They worshipped creation in the most direct way, seven thousand years ago. This is the first real proof we've got that the Mother Goddess did rule once, before Zeus. The feminists are right, after all.'

Even after all the mayhem Lucan had not given up goddesses altogether.

Sonia came down to the shop the following morning. 'I hear you saw Lucan last night?' She cast a long, level look.

Lillian felt flattered. This conqueror was jealous.

Sonia sat on the book table, spreading her skirts, preparing to perform. 'Angus makes a fetish of Katherine. Every time he sits with a group of her admirers he turns it into a seance.'

She leant further forward. 'Everywhere he goes. Every time he meets influential people. He promotes her. He resurrects her. He's creating a global fan-club for her. It's vile. Do you know what she used to do?'

Lillian waited for some bizarre or shameful revelation, smelling Sonia's Joie perfume, Roger et Gallet soap and the faint stench of the swamp.

'She used to mark out all the Russian lessons on the Third Programme in the *Radio Times*. She'd clip them together and hang them on the kitchen wall.' Sonia put her hand on Lillian's cardigan, and her husky voice took on a new, raucous note. 'She'd never miss a lesson. She was obsessional.'

Sonia had been driven mad by this tiny detail of her dead rival's competence. She stared down at Lillian.

'Angus's praise of Katherine is perfectly justified. She's a genius!'

Sonia was jealous, not only of Katherine's talent and fame, but also of the mysterious power her death had given her. She was jealous of her death.

SIXTEEN

The first-class return ticket to Paris which Bernard had so shrewdly sent to her sat on the mantelpiece in her flat until the date of departure, which was a Saturday. At eleven in the morning she was planting seedlings in the windowbox which no one had taken any care of since Josh's mysterious defection. She found his little green trowel, now chipped. Holding the trowel made her sad. She peered at the gardening dirt under her fingernails. The plane was due to take off for Orly airport in two hours.

At Orly, Bernard's face was tighter than ever. Was her arrival a blight? Was it only her indifference that attracted him? He had checked her into a hotel in the Rue du Tournon. He took her for an aperitif in the Marais so that she could admire the buildings. For dinner he bought her salmon and lemon mousse at Maxim's. Later they went to a bistro in Contrescarpe where she could listen to the calculated romanticism of the French chanteuse. When he danced with her on the handkerchief floor, he held her at a distance as if she were a blood relative.

At four in the morning he delivered her to her hotel. She flopped, fully clothed, on the bed, idly turning on the hotel radio, hoping for some jazz. She was beyond exhaustion, wide-awake, observant. Ready for a *nuit-blanche*. She began to pick the dirt from under her fingernails.

Bernard sat stiffly on the Louis XIV chair in his formal clothes. She didn't want him, but she wanted to assuage him, because he was there.

'Come over here,' she said.

In the morning when he sat up, thinking of breakfast, she reclaimed him. A shade of irritation crossed his face. But he glanced quickly at his watch. '*Oui, maintenant pour quelques moments de tendresse.*' She should have been warned.

And when he munched his croissant, he chewed, not with his back molars, but with his endlessly polished front teeth. To avoid the irritation she looked down at the boulevard. The café umbrellas seen from above had shiny patches from a recent rainfall. Wrought-iron gates curved enticingly into court-yards. She would like to prowl the city on her own.

But when they walked across the Luxembourg Gardens, his arm around her shoulder, trailing his jacket, she felt the delight of his protection. Even the small espaliered vines, over-trained, over-controlled like Bernard, took on a certain novel radiance.

Whenever she peered closely at his face she became absorbed in its minutiae. But from a distance, watching him walk to the corner to buy *Le Monde*, he seemed stiff, insignificant.

But he wooed with surprising vigour. The rush of adrenalin made his dark hair curl into beguiling ringlets, his blue eyes glint. Once, his head in her lap, he looked up at her and the new-born blueness of his eyes gave her hope. Perhaps there was something he would yield up to her. He was so calm about sex. It was like eating artichokes.

He wanted to annoy his mother by choosing this unlikely bride. And besides, he'd fallen for her. He liked her moody face. But he did not fully gauge the machinery of yearning she carted about inside her. He tried Aznavour on her, but she found that mushy. He tried poetry, lifting up a tress of her hair: 'Much have I travelled in the realms of gold,' he intoned, in his French accent. That worked.

SEVENTEEN

Bernard installed her in a magnificent flat off Place St Michel. But, like an air-plant, she had to draw all her oxygen through her leaves. She had no roots here. So she became a boulevardier, inhaling all of Paris and its incorrigible Frenchness. In Montparnasse cafés, she was soon recognized as a chronic drifter, one of them. Despite her references to her husband, her children.

On Sunday they would take the children to visit Bernard's mother in Neuilly, carrying boxes of cakes tied up in elaborate bows. He would point out the bullet-marks on the sides of buildings where the Germans shot resistance fighters, while the children touched the indentations trying to separate in their minds all the wars and revolutions. History was a river of blood, bridged with dates. Sometimes Lillian looked at Bernard's framed photograph of Jean Moulin, standing in a doorway, scarf flying, half-smiling, doomed, and felt an old romantic impulse. There were millions of them killed. Women's other halves.

In the creaking apartment, a pained Bernard would go through the motions (in bed and out of bed he went through the motions), handing his sons to his mother to keep her quiet. Lillian, well-shod now, not bad at French, would stare out of the long windows, watching the long afternoon apparently stand still. Green buses below, still with their tantalizing foreignness. A boy, with unbrushed hair hurried by, his arm around a girl. What were they running towards?

Then the light would change. Jerome would touch her face. His ardour was as beautiful as the sea. Fabrice even made the old lady relent, reciting Victor Hugo without a word wrong. Nectarines would be brought in. Peppermints. The light through the shutters stippled the fruit; shimmered with immanence. Australia was miles away. England, a seedy love story.

Katherine Feldmann's suicide became myth. The sales of her books increased and she became set reading in most American and English literary courses. Theses were written about her work and many books.

A rash of suicides among sensitive women broke out. Many of them had in their possession a copy of the *Collected Works*. These women were kamikaze pilots in the just-brewing sex war.

Felicity telephoned. She and Robert were on their way back from a holiday in the Ardeche. They had to wait for the next train in the Gare du Nord. Should they meet for dinner?

Robert looked better; his bottle shoulders sagged less. It was amazing what fresh air and excercise could do for you. A spot of healthy selfishness. But Felicity had the look of someone who tolerated going abroad for her husband's sake.

After the meal Robert and Bernard went out to the station to check in the bags before departure. The women were to follow. Lillian watched them walk away, both good providers. An image of Josh (his strength) and Lucan (his glamour) came to her mind. Did people ever get the ones they wanted?

'Bernard looks more and more like Pierre Cardin. You're lucky, Lillian.'

'His clothes all have Cardin labels, too. He's grown to resemble their maker.'

'Are you okay, Lillian? You seem subdued.'

'Oh, it's marriage I suppose. You rub along, but you don't know what's biting the other. Marriage doesn't seem to be about passion at all much, does it?'

'Oh, on and off.'

'But passion keeps you alive. It's so invigorating. It's where art comes from too, I think.'

'Also murder. Let's talk about something more cheerful.' Felicity picked up the little packets of sugar and slipped them into her pocket for the children. 'How are your kids? Aren't you glad you had Jerome now?'

Too soon after the birth of Fabrice, Lillian, pregnant again, sneaked over to London for an abortion and stayed with Felicity. But at the hospital a woman doctor, in mid examination straightened up and looked into her eyes.

'It's positioned so beautifully . . . it seems a shame . . .'

Lillian burst into a crying fit.

'Look, I don't think you've really made up your mind.' The doctor peeled off her plastic gloves. 'Go home and think about it.' Felicity opened her front door to a laughing Lillian. 'I couldn't go through with it.'

'That doctor was psychic. Jerome is my consolation. He's so warm and cuddly. I'm wildly in love with him. How's Sonia?' she asked suddenly.

'You know she had a lump on her breast?'

'Oh God.'

'I visited her in hospital. They had made her sign a form to agree to surgery on her breast if it was thought necessary. And you know what that means! For our love-goddess. Anyway, it all turned out fine.'

'I suppose Lucan was there?'

'Well, that's the odd part. She asked me to ring him, to tell him the news. She gave me a country number. Very remote. He was in Scotland on some new dig. You have to go through the local switchboard, you know, where the girls knit and listen. So conversation can't exactly flow. He said, "Hullo". I said, "Hullo, I've got some marvellous news for you." He was silent. Absolutely silent. Although he must have known what was coming. I thought I'd been cut off. "Sonia is okay. The lump isn't malignant." And do you know what his comment was when he eventually deigned to make one?'

'What?'

'He said, "I see. Now perhaps she'll stop playing La Dame aux Camellias." '

Lillian stared down at her coffee, repressing a smile.

'I begged him to phone her, and do you know what that extraordinary man said? He said, "Why?" Just like that, "Why?" "You must ring her," I said. "I don't see the necessity." That's all I could get out of him.'

Lillian laughed. But something in her was still fascinated by Lucan's imperviousness.

She soon gave up trying to please Bernard. No matter how hard she manicured and marinated there was still something unkempt about her; a wildness, about everything she did.

'My hair's gone mousy,' she'd say. 'But it'll come back, like it was, given time.'

Bernard did not live by tidal changes. He was a measured person. Driving back to France after a furniture-buying foray, Bernard and Lillian stopped in a Seville bar where an American girl with long, blonde hair, the kind Bernard called 'professor-traps', was eating dried fish with one hand and holding the *Collected Works* with the other. Snatches of flamenco sung from the kitchen floated around the air like torn, red taffeta. Men in formal business suits were reading Spanish newspapers, smoking and playing dominoes, having fun, far away from their cloistered wives. The American girl cried, for the absent wives, perhaps, into the open pages of the *Collected Works*.

In a Marseilles pavement bar having a milkshake (a pang of homesickness for Australia), while Bernard gazed impatiently at his watch, Lillian saw a woman of late middle-age emerge from a tourist bus holding the *Collected Works*, gripping it tighter than her handbag.

In Florence, in an exquisite villa, Bernard and Lillian watched the sunset soften the Fuseli vineyards in apricot down. The hostess read out Katherine Feldmann's long, bitter diatribe about male betrayal in the presence of her poker-faced husband.

Walking back to the Ledra Palace in Nicosia a Greek Orthodox priest made the sign of the devil's horns when he saw her red hair glinting. Over an electric water-pump in a nearby village she saw a goat's skull propped up to ward off the demon that made the pump break down. In the Turkish quarter where they ate a dish called Ladies Thighs, a veiled woman was poring over Katherine Feldmann's *Collected Works*.

EIGHTEEN

From her tall, shuttered windows you could see down into the gardens of the deaf-and-dumb institute. A fountain skeined water into silver fronds. Intensities of green ranged from the lime of the willow shoots to the perennial hedge. Sometimes the afflicted wandered about the formal garden, honking to each other in the strange owl-cry of the dumb.

Lillian stood there, in the shadows of the shutter, yet clearly visible to them all. She wanted to take off her clothes and stand there, letting the breeze play over her nakedness, rampant and shameful. She wanted that. But she was giving a dinner party for eight. And Bernard had been upset last time because she had run out of bread. The French can't eat a meal without bread. She pulled herself away from the shutters and went to the boulangerie.

On a rare Autumn day, when well-being flowed regardless, Lillian was in the courtyard planting basil. She almost didn't answer the telephone. Let it ring. It'll only be a bore. Bernard's mother most likely. A mirror-image of Bernard. A stickler for details.

She answered it still in gardening gloves. The call was from London.

'Felicity! Are you coming over darling?'

'No.'

She waited.

'Felicity?'

'Lillian. Oh Christ, fucking hell!'

The breathing was heavy. Then a sob broke, like a bubble.

The line crackled in her ear. It sounded like the time she had swum out too far. Got the ocean in her middle ear.

'How are you Felicity?' Lillian's voice had taken on an anxious note.

'Sonia is dead.'

'Sonia!' Not Sonia! Lillian stared at her gardening gloves; her hand resting on the cedarwood of the piano.

'She shot herself.'

'My God!'

'I've just been to the funeral. I sat next to Lucan. He was crying all the time.'

They'd finally got him to cry.

Lillian went upstairs and lay on the bed, staring at the Gustave Doré prints that seeped with the pleasures of melancholy, the eroticism of thwarted passion. She could not pretend to be grieving. But she was shocked. She listened attentively to the bootless cries of the deaf-and-dumb, as if trying to interpret them.

Sonia, so greedy for everything; such a frenzied and cunning struggler.

NINETEEN

In the Select Café, a beam of wayward sun flashed back from her coffee spoon amid the dimness of potted palms, brass urns and posters. This was the mood she liked best in Montparnasse. Only the most tenacious and secretive of bums turned up at this hour for their coffee. They were, for the moment, off duty.

At night the same bar would be full of professional pimps and cruisers. The general contempt which was the set expression of the waiters, by day, became satanic around midnight.

At this time of day the customers gave each other lots of room.

Lillian chose the corner. The three tables on her right were mercifully vacant. The next was occupied by the twins.

These two dark men in tall white hats always wore identical black suits. It had been rumoured that when the twins were small they were incarcerated in a German concentration camp and that they now lived, doing no work all day, on government compensation.

They always nodded to her when she arrived, just as she nodded to the Yugoslav pimp, who had told her so many lies about the beauty of his childhood in Dubrovnik.

The others were strangers to her. As usual the expatriates stuck together.

She stared at the pages of the *Herald Tribune* to look busy. She wanted to be in neutral surroundings away from the *froideur* of her own house, its endless commands, where beef was marinating for Bernard's dinner.

A Japanese businessman at the bar was looking at her legs, at her foreign hair burnished like the brass urns. She opened her bag and took out her mirror. Her face wasn't so bad. She was still on that plateau women enter at about thirty. Sonia had been growing older. Her forties were upon here. Her beauty must have been flagging, slipping out of her. Lillian put away her mirror. No, it wouldn't have been fading beauty that made Sonia shoot herself.

She folded her paper and nodded to the twins who were just leaving. She left a few francs on the little brass dish and went downstairs to the Ladies.

She made her way down the Rue Vavin and bought six lemon tarts at the better of the two cake shops. She also bought some quiche which she'd heat up for lunch.

Balancing these on open palms she crossed into the Luxembourg Gardens.

Sitting down in the spindly chairs, contemplating the bust of Baudelaire bearded in dark green leaves were the twins, their black suits and hats casting paler shadows on the lawn.

They nodded and she returned the salute. They had been in Belsen, and they were alive and well on spindly chairs in the Luxembourg. They were the meek. Unlike Sonia.

She walked through the gardens, through columns of chestnuts; their shadow striping the whitish dust. Concierges ate fat cakes at the kiosk. Children sped around on the merry-go-round, trying to hook a prize as they whirled. Some did. Some didn't.

She sat on the edge of the fountain, looking at banks of flowers; statues of dead queens; aware that someone was watching her.

Still balancing her patisserie, she stood up, and made off towards the Boulevard St Michel.

The man touched her shoulder. She turned round and saw Albert Camus. He had that curly hair, those amused, intelligent eyes.

'*Excusez-moi Madame, mais je voudrais parler avec vous pour quelques minutes.*'

'*Non, monsieur,*' she replied at once. '*Je suis en train de rencontrer mon mari et mes six enfants.*'

She walked on briskly, triumphantly, as if she had won a contest. Then looked down at her arm, goosepimply with a kind of deprivation. She glanced back, to call him back, but the man had vanished forever.

Despising her cowardice, her endless cloddish pride, she opened the chipped grey door into the seventeenth-century courtyard, stooped to pick a sprig of tarragon.

Fabrice, home early, was playing a Chopin mazurka, which pleased her. Part of his recent sulkiness – a preview of adolescence, she supposed – had been giving up things he was good at, things he knew gave her satisfaction. Like the piano.

The sudden rush of Chopin was a cheerful sign. From upstairs she could hear the singing of the new maid who stole her perfume.

She turned the beef in the marinade and began to chop garlic into tiny pieces. Bernard was due home for dinner. All this cooking kept women out of mischief; away from covens and cabals and secret uprisings.

She wanted to go over and touch her first born but was

afraid he'd shrug her off. For years they were in love with you. Then suddenly you became physically repulsive. Was that the drama husbands had to re-enact with their wives?

But there was more to it. Her son was so angry with the veil of unease in the house she was afraid all his hair would start to fall out. The youngest, Jerome, who had always been so demonstrative, had lately withdrawn, coldly absorbed in his construction toys.

'Felicity, should I leave him?' she asked on a late-night phone call to her best friend. 'All I need is to gather the energy. He has such control. I can't penetrate it.'

'You are too used to each other,' replied Felicity, always the little home-maker. 'It could have been much worse. Bernard is just reserved. Reticent.'

Then forgive us our reticences.

She unfolded the best white lace tablecloth and spread it over the oak table. In the centre she put the large blue jug crammed with fluttering poppies in every shade of yellow and red. The long fruit basket Bernard had bought her in San Gimignano was laden with tight-skinned nectarines. She set out the Victorian plates with the pale green flower pattern. Bernard had bought the dinner service in Wales and presented it to her with a flourish.

The Chopin covered the house in ripples. From upstairs she could hear the voice of the Portuguese maid singing about love. How envied we must be, going south every August, skiing in February, living here, for years and years, with the deaf-and-dumb fountain glistening away outside.

TWENTY

When she was with Felicity, on her shopping visits to London, they might still be back in their old flat. There was the ease, the giggling and the endless musing over moral issues. They raved on.

'But, Felicity, you could get cancer, not expressing your anger.'

'Health isn't all it's cracked up to be. Hitler was healthy, wasn't he?'

It was cosy stuff. They were friends forever. She could feel a sort of shifting of her skin when she entered Felicity's house, put down her bundles. But marriages were mysterious, even to the participants.

Whenever she asked Felicity about Robert, a vague look passed over her thin face; it was as if she were trying to tune into some foreign station. 'Oh good old Robert. Never stops working. He told me he married me because I wouldn't complain. The truth is I don't notice much, if he's here or not.'

'But what do you do when the kids are at school? I've been doing more journalism.'

'You've forgotten I teach twice a week at The Morley. English and typing. It's totally exhausting.'

'So we both have our little hobbies.'

'When we got married, we had children. We didn't want to palm them off. We were crazy about them.'

'Hmm. I think those affairs are coming to an end.'

Supper at Felicity's. The garden tapping on the window its annual consolation prize. A prized cat grooming her privates on top of the piano no one played. The boys had given up trying. Only Lillian on her periodic visits played *Fur Elise*. There were no dramatic chords any more. No tears on the ivories.

'There's a programme on Katherine Feldmann tonight on TV. We must watch it. You met her, didn't you?'

'Not exactly,' said Lillian.

At the cooker, heating up pizzas; at the sink washing lettuce; Felicity wavered. Her fingers were often pink with burn-marks, scabbed from old tin-opener wounds. She didn't look after herself. Lillian brought her some jokey pot-holders from France. Felicity hung them on a hook and forgot about them, grabbing at worn teatowels when she needed protection, then burning herself on the dish half-way between cooker and table. She'd shake her hand vaguely and suck it. She seemed disassociated from her own body.

Robert was invariably late. He arrived when the boys were bolting their food, behind a carapace of comics. Like his wife, he was not a gourmet. He asked Lillian about Paris as if it was a sick relative; for Robert the only significant geography consisted of a few streets off Ladbroke Grove. There he knew every manhole, every peeled doorway. But tonight he made an effort; opened a bottle.

'When are you coming back to London? You belong here, you know.' He spoke, softly, as if he was telling her a secret.

Yes, if friendship counted, this was home. Australia was smells and colours, rolling in the dust, adolescent boredom.

'It's on the cards. Bernard has agreed.' Lillian picked a bit of cork from her lip. The cat sprang on to the keys, making a discordant sound, reminding her of pain.

'There's a TV programme on Katherine Feldmann tonight. She and Sonia were friends, before . . . ' Felicity hesitated.

'Before Sonia stole her man,' laughed Robert. Sonia. Her hair had reminded him of a net; trawling; she was a fisher of men.

'No, I'm going to have a daub.' But he looked away, embarrassed at his own pretension.

The programme was the usual paeon to a dead artist. A professor talked about that day Katherine Feldmann came to his house to interview him for a woman's magazine. He admitted that he had not realized that the chirpy journalist in the tartan skirt was a genius. 'There still remains an ambiguous element to her suicide,' he said.

Lillian felt cold, locked in ice.

THE DESCENT OF EROS

TWENTY-ONE

Billie Holliday is singing on the radio and Lillian is picking up a safety-pin, rusted brown by sea-air, when there is a knock at the door.

She props her broom up and edges down the hall crammed with broken chairs and a massive, dusty hall-stand. The obstacles which slow her progress also give her time to be cautious.

'Who is it?'

Silence.

'Who is it?'

'Open the door.'

'Who *is* it?'

'I want to show you something.' The voice is slow and crawling.

'Are you the new tenant downstairs?'

'Just open the door lady and don't come the lah-de-dah with me.'

'I certainly will not.'

The door starts to shake. It's made of the cheapest plywood and is weakened by age and sea air.

'When I'm *ready*, I'll come down and speak to you.'

She hears him clump downstairs. Then the banging on his ceiling starts, reverberating at her feet. She expects to see the broom handle sticking up through the floorboards. Penile and menacing. But she turns down the Billie Holliday. At times like this you need a man around. She remembers Bruiser upstairs.

With her lopsided broom she bangs on her ceiling. He must be up there. He retires early because of the dawn shift.

She settles down to wait for him, thinking of Bernard, twenty-five thousand kilometres away. He would have disposed neatly of the man downstairs. One phone call and he'd be collected by the men in white.

At the next knock she hastens to open the door, hoping to see Bruiser's battered face, but keeps the chain on, in case.

'Take the chain off, bitch.'

The man downstairs is back, red-faced and armed. His eyes are a dead white.

'Go away, will you.'

'Look lady. You're provoking me. I'm sick of people like you. You should be put down.'

The gun nozzle is pointing at her stomach. She dodges sideways.

'I don't give a shit. But before I die I can rid the world of tarts like you.'

She bangs the door in his bloated face.

'I'm calling the police now.' She enunciates each word slowly and loudly. He probably hadn't bargained on her having a phone. He would only attack women who are well and truly cornered.

She sighs. The trouble with living in a cheap stinking lodging-house by the sea is that flotsam like him blow in, along with the fish-and-chip paper and the dented Cola cans that skid into the corridor at the slightest gust of wind.

It's worse when the tail-end of a typhoon lashes down from Darwin, like now. The sea goes a towering grey. There are no more orderly waves, just turbulence.

'So what did the police do when they came?' asks her nephew, in town for the evening. They are at the opening of an art exhibition. He has met her at the gallery as arranged, but with him is Simon, who had been using her balcony for weeks now to park his board.

'Nothing the police could do. They went downstairs, and he pitched them some sob-story about dying of heart disease. Then they informed me, with due solemnity, that he had Been Through the Pacific.'

'Has the prick bothered you again?'

'Oh, whenever I leave the house, he lurks down there with his carpet-sweeper. The local kids chant, "There goes the bad man", which doesn't help. He even kicks dogs.'

'Bastard,' says Simon. He is sitting too close to her on a low dais underneath a huge, inextricable mass of metal balanced on a plinth. They have all drunk far too much free champagne.

Flunkeys hand round plates of prunes skewered on bits of bacon. The premier's wife gives a pep-talk about the flourishing state of art in Australia. The other women have similar long, blonde hair drawn back and large, tinted glasses. It's the usual assortment of overdressed women with too few escorts.

The men who aren't homosexual, who have deigned to come to this cultural event have the look of some rare object that must be closely guarded. The missing escorts are in the pubs, chalking pool sticks, downing pints, being slugged. Or in some hinterland between the two.

'Go off and flirt with the girls,' Lillian says to her young men airily. 'They need you.' Her nephew duly obeys, padding off for an easy killing.

But Simon remains gallantly at her side, sipping champagne. Light shines from under his skin. She feels millions of tiny electrical filaments pulling at her skin pores.

'Well, if you're going to be my troubadour, how about some more champagne?' How arch I am. A faded old cocotte.

But all evening, he stays with her, apart from trying to find the man with the tray. Shy probably, she tells herself. After all, he's at home with me. He's seen me slopping about in Manly.

But he has started to stare at her. 'You know, I've been looking at you all night. You really fit in here. Dressed up like that.'

She smiles.

He tells her she always seems happy. She says she often gets depressed . . . and she runs her hand from ear to ear. 'I mean, if I get deprived enough . . .'

What was she up to? Fishing for sympathy. Signalling need. Knowing that otherwise he would be too intimidated to approach her. Funny, she could reach out so easily for affection from a woman or a boy. Men, though, that's a different story.

Simon opens his eyes. Some of the sea has escaped into his irises. He gives her that trusting look that makes her afraid. He could die a cot-death if she wasn't careful.

Now they are driving home across town, with him breathing behind her. They pause at the lights for an impatient few seconds, the car bucking like a horse. She stares at a brightly lit shop window. On display is a huge photograph of Katherine Feldmann, taken on a picnic, hair tumbling; a laughing mouth, wide and lucky.

She pretends to be drunker than she is. Her head flops back on the seat. She is giggly.

Her nephew is driving too fast, tossing twenty cents into the bridge toll, missing, speeding off to the sound of alarm bells.

The night wind rushes past on its broomstick, and the trees in suburban gardens writhe. She looks up at the stars hoping to see one fall, but moves her eyes too soon and gets only the tail-end of a wish. The surfer's hands are touching her hair.

A million tiny crystals of pleasure break out on her scalp, sending up tingling waves. His hands lift her hair, separating it into love-locks.

She says with fortitude to her nephew's profile above the wheel, 'Your flirtatious friend is giving me a head massage.'

'Good for him.'

She collapses back, succumbing to the bliss. She is deprived all right. Touch-deprived. For twenty minutes or so her head is on fire; her hair tangled in his fingers.

The boys escort her upstairs 'in case that loony bastard downstairs is waiting up for you'.

'He won't know what hit him.'

'A jab to the solar plexus and a knife blow to the back of the neck, and then we'll throw him over North Head.' Yep, what you need is muscle.

Inside the flat she searches rather a long time for wine and glasses. Her heart is noisy, drawing too much attention to itself.

When Simon goes out of the room her nephew winks at her.

'Don't be ridiculous. I'm old enough to be his grandmother,' she snaps and sets down the glasses with a bang.

'Well, one of us has got to stay here with you tonight to protect you, and it can't be me, Aunty dear.'

When he drives off, the two of them sit out on the balcony. But the wind is so wild it blows down the surfboard every time he straightens it against the wall.

'Bring it inside. Maybe you can go surfing tomorrow.'

'No, the sewage will be all washed in.'

Inside, she attempts a distancing motherly stance. She sits opposite him, quizzing him about his work, even his dreams.

'I dream about women.'

He didn't say girls, he said women. She wishes he wasn't young. She wishes he was a hundred. But he's here, and he's looking at her with eyes that make her afraid.

Omitting to bid him a terminal goodnight, she retires to her bedroom and lies there in the dark with the door open. That's the trouble with falling stars, they fall just as you're turning away, and you only get the tail-end of a wish.

She lies on the bed listening to music in the dark. But even the lunatic downstairs can't possibly hear it because the wind is blowing the world about. She has an impression that everything is colliding.

A dark figure appears at her door. 'Can I crash here?'

Simon drops down beside her. They lie motionless, staring out at the black sea. She has left the door to the balcony wide open. The room is full of spray. They're on a raft together, drifting towards The Heads.

She puts an arm around him cosily and remembers putting her arm on Terry for the first time. The reflexive jerk of a corpse. But this is different. This time she won't cry tears of surprise. She has been making love to this particular god all her life.

After a few minutes she turns her face and the kissing starts, tangled with the odour of hyacinths from the flowerpot beside them.

Of course, adolescents . . . lots of ears and neck. She sits up briskly and unzips, unhooks. 'I feel like Mrs Robinson.'

'Simon and Garfunkel wrote that.'

They are both naked. The only light that touches them comes from the shimmer the sea throws up. She's pleased about the discretion of the sea light. They make love all over the flat, even standing up in the shower where the cockroaches scuttle.

The sea roars like a heart heard on a megaphone. All night the huge heart-beat fills the room, blowing pine needles into corners and rusting dropped pins.

'I feel as if I'd thrown a net over the balcony in the night and hauled up a salamander,' she tells him.

He half-lies on her bed, netted in gold. It's the street light striking through the pine branches. He is leaning on her with the back of his head on her breasts. They are both looking towards the sea, silver lights corkscrewing off breakers.

His shoulders are dark on her unsunned skin. Round his throat his horoscope chain glints silver. She is frightened to speak of most things in case it frightens him off: her age, her chequered past that lies out there as silently as a nuclear submarine, her two sons on the other side of the world.

It's the hour of the wolf. The time between night and dawn. The same level of dark exists now on the other side of the world. Between dusk and night. At this hour ghosts walk. And if she walked into her home in London, by the turning light, she might mistake that post-dusk for this pre-dawn. Her sons must hear her footfall now, her sigh, the rattle of filial chains.

She holds Simon and remains silent.

'You never know what she's going to do,' he says, breaking the silence.

'Who?'

'The *sea*.'

'Ah.'

'She's different every time.' He leans up on his elbow and reaches for a glass. 'No two waves are ever the same. It's better than climbing, not so predictable. The mountains move.'

She sits up and sips too, knowing she looks radiant by starlight. Her body is perfect. Perfect. It has been renewed.

'There's a rock out there where we surf by the reef. Surge Rock. Sometimes it's covered by water. You can't see it. Then it's deadly. Other times it sticks up, plainly visible.'

'Probably connected with the tides.'

'No, that's the strange thing, Lillian. It isn't. It just sometimes appears. Nothing to do with tides or the swell. We all have to watch out for it.'

'Have any surfies struck it?'

'Don't say surfies, say surfers,' he admonishes.

She reminds herself that he is eighteen, old enough, yes, to be her third son. The lucky third.

She steels herself to make a grim remark, to drop a scalding drop on his shimmering flesh. 'I can't be seen out with you. We can't go anywhere together, you know.'

'You're so conventional, beautiful lady.'

'Breakfast at Sweethearts,' he says, taking the plate of eggs and bacon on to the bed. It is the name of a pop song. He knows all their names, all their words. She looks away. Maybe he'll notice the lines around her eyes . . . her dishpan hands . . . her . . .

'You wouldn't know there'd been a storm last night. The sewage all went the other way.'

He goes over the road for a dip, and she waves to him, confident in her beauty, from a distance. He is the black silhouette riding his board with his arms out like a descending angel.

She is the woman on the balcony with the sun-glint on her hair.

That angel on the surfboard, he's my lover.

When he leaves the sea, he stops at the tap on the esplanade and rinses himself all over, shaking off the water like a puppy.

She knows she doesn't deserve it. It is an accident. It will go away. She blinks harshly at the cockroaches, unable to kill them.

He stays with her all morning, waxing his board, informing her about pop songs. She always seems to have sand in the sheets.

Late one night he knocks. He has a book under his arm. *In Praise of Older Women* by Stephen Vizinczey. He has the eager look of a student embarking on a course. She wonders if she should tell him that she has met the author.

'I've brought you a present.' He hands her a wooden pepper mill. 'I was sick of seeing you pouring pepper out of a packet. Not you.'

He produces two bottles of claret from a plastic bag. 'Dad thought I'd gone to bed, but I climbed out of the window and raided his cellar.' He was showering her with gifts.

He is at that age when not enough happens, and he can give his all to her. They are two waves colliding. Hers going down. His going up. They meet in foam.

Later, looking up into the darkness, one arm under his head, he says, 'I think we've got caught in a time-warp.'

He runs to see her all the way from his parents' bungalow because he has no money for the bus fare. He runs in the driving rain, stopping to tear up municipal marigolds from Manly Corso. She opens the door to his drenched figure; his flowers and his kisses in a big bunch under his chin.

'How romantic!' But there is no one she can confide in. Not a soul. She has not had time to make friends. And even if she could confide, how would it sound? 'Last night an eighteen-year-old boy of surpassing beauty ran five kilometres in the rain to present me with a posy of marigolds.' They are dancing a tango in the sky. They are clouds. But there is no one to marvel at them, only themselves.

TWENTY-TWO

'Good waves today,' she says, not looking at him. The light is cruelly bright, so she turns her head away and picks up the vase of white chrysanthemums to make room for the breakfast tray.

'Hey! Wait a minute!' Simon reaches out and takes the flower with the broken stem out of the vase. 'I'm keeping this. Forever.'

Last night she had taken that flower from its vase and brushed it with a spider's lightness over his body. Very slowly she had brushed the tips of its petals on the soles of his feet, ankles, calves, shins, thighs, cock . . . on his eyelids, ears, cheeks, forehead, lips, chest, arms, diaphragm, stomach . . . and brushed all down his back.

'I'll press it in the leaves of a book,' he grins.

Ah. Souvenirs already. Like her, he has a sense that it's too good to last. It will be a memory so astonishing that proofs will be needed.

On the tray there's the usual scrambled eggs with a sprig of parsley on top, plus bacon. 'Why do you always cut the toast diagonally? I'll always remember that about you.'

'I hope you'll remember a few other things,' she says, flashing him a look, willing him to see only her good points.

He laughs, but still doesn't sit up, lying there twirling the broken flower in his hand, one arm under his head. Around his neck there are several purple love bites.

She has love bites too, but you can't see them under her clothes.

She takes her plate out of the room, to eat on the balcony.

Let him lie languorously. She'd look at sterner stuff; the power-shovels roaring along the tide-marks, cleaning up seaweed and bluebottles and bits of plastic before the trippers come; the old husband of the Filipino girl hauling in a crate of frozen chips from a van.

As if in compensation for her nightly visitant, the daytime has taken on a harsher character. The article on Ananda Marga was turned down by the editor with no explanation. She fears he is thinking of dispensing with her. Funny how you can always tell. She has been too reasonable in her defence of them. She must re-write.

But she doesn't want to lift a finger. She wants to go back to bed. With him.

'Come back to bed woman,' he shouts, reading her thoughts. After all, he'd got into her blood.

'I've got work to do lazybones.'

There is silence. She hears his feet thump on the floor. The clatter of knife and fork.

She enters the bedroom, her back to the light. 'Look, I've got time to walk with you to Shelley Beach. You'll be surfing there today, I suppose?'

He puts on his shorts and thongs. He's dressed. It takes five seconds. But first he wants to listen to his Dire Straits record. She's getting to like it.

> The conductress on the No. 19
> She was a honey,
> Pink toenails and hands
> All dirty with her money.

Walking towards Shelley Beach they come face to face with the ubiquitous Bruiser. He is sweeping the front, as usual.

As they approach, not touching but with no air-pocket between them, so even the birds would know they were aligned, Bruiser rests on his broom, shaking his head with mock disapproval.

'It's a great life for *some*, if you don't have to work.'

'I'd like your job,' says Simon. 'Soaking up the sun all day. Taking a dip now and then. Being paid for it.'

'Yeah. How about cleaning out the toilets? You wouldn't like that now, wouldyer?'

Simon smiles. He has only just left school. He keeps telling himself he can still be unemployed for a while without feeling desperate.

Bruiser peers at the purple marks on his neck. 'Someone's been havin' a go atyer, mate.'

Lillian darts on ahead. When Simon joins her he is smiling. 'I'm sure he knows the sex maniac is you.'

'No, no, he'll think it's some bathing beauty. Not an old hag like me.'

'You're beautiful.'

'Yes. In a way,' she says bitterly and turns to gaze at the purple lantana tumbling down the cliff, inextricably mixed with the common glamour of nasturtiums.

On Shelley Beach he puts down his board and kicks off his

thongs. Other surfers are out there already, gleaming blackly in their wet-suits like a school of sharks. She can only bear to dart quick glimpses of Simon for fear of being dazzled. The boys of her generation had not been like him. There was nothing mystic in their attitude to the sea. They liked to get your head down and duck you, touching your budding breasts accidentally on purpose. Or else they showed off on the high diving board, going out slowly on to the coconut-matting, standing on tip-toe, extending their arms, breathing in deeply so their ribs stuck out, their solar-plexuses extended; holding the pose of Apollo in majesty.

'He has a lovely physique. He's a dreamboat,' the girls would murmur.

One of the black sharks waves to Simon. He waves back. Lillian turns quickly. 'I should be going to work.'

'Okay. Seeyer later alligator. Hey, look, there's Surge Rock. It was covered yesterday.'

'It's safer when you can see it, I suppose.'

'One day I'll solve the mystery.' He laughs the laugh of the unfallen.

But she notices a broken capillary by his nostril curve. Alcoholism is waiting for him, like a bully behind a bush. And beyond that the spectre of Failure, because Simon is too dreamy, too lazy, too sensual to study, to deny himself, to make plans.

The Flame tree gives a restless shade. A mongrel sniffs around the remains of yesterday's barbecues. A lone Japanese child swings upside down on the squeaking swing.

'I like it under this tree. It's a "power-place".' When she departs, he lies back on the sand. The sun stamps on his eyelids, even through the tree-shade.

In the distance the Manly megaphone chants its diurnal message.

'Move further north all board riders, or your boards will be impounded for one month.'

The sergeant-major voice is angrier than usual today, itching to put an end to their happiness.

The older life-savers do not like these surfers with their vague, distant gaze, their sun-bleached locks, their loping, unregimented walks. Spoiled dole-bludgers. They'd never have to go to war. Would always get Social Security. Could fuck without getting a girl pregnant. Could laze about on the sand all day, bloody beach bums.

Someone throws sand at him. 'Hey mate, is it true you're in love with your best friend's Aunty?'

'Who said that?'

'Is it true?'

'What do you think?'

'You give me the shits. Where've you been lately, anyway?'

'Around.'

'Getting your end away?'

'One-track mind.'

'Maybe you're a poofter, pretty enough for one.'

Laughter.

'There's a party tonight at the Surf Club. Three girls coming over from Narrabeen. There'll be a queue. Coming? We'll see if you're a poofter or not.'

'Maybe.'

'Got a job yet?'

'Three interviews coming up. A bakery. A garage. A factory.'

'You'll soon get fed up. Then we'll steal a van and go up north. My Uncle's got an avocado farm.' He kicks the prone body before him until its springs up and they wrestle on the sand.

Lillian is almost around the headland, but she pauses by the rock pool where an old lady in a bathing cap and rubber shoes does her daily twenty lengths. She glances back at the beach and sees Simon struggling with his friend on the shore. Two young puppies.

Every fourth or fifth wave is a big one. It jets its foam further up the beach, over their romping bodies. It's hard to imagine them middle-aged, full of rancour and contradictions, cooking spare-ribs over a suburban barbecue; reverting to type.

A feeling presses down on her. It is her duty to leave him to his own generation.

She can see the danger. It is plainly visible. Like Surge Rock.

She waits at the top of the stairs ready to go into town, listening to her enemy below. He is sweeping and sweeping that same bit of hall floor, waiting to attack with his carpet-sweeper.

She runs up to Bruiser's door. He often slips back inside to pour himself a cool drink from his fridge.

He sees her at the door and flushes with pleasure. She scuttles in.

'Now I *know* you like 'em young, dontcher?'

When she stiffens he says, 'Whaddyer think of me white rug, sweetie? Got all modern conveniences. Everything you'll ever need.' He glances roguishly down at his cock.

'Bruiser, *please*, come with me when I go downstairs. I can't walk by his door unescorted. He'll murder me.'

'He's harmless. I told that to them two nurses out the back. He just doesn't like women. Beats me. Anyway, you gotta make allowances; he's been through the Pacific.'

'Fuck the Pacific. He drew a knife on my friend. And he's got a gun. I banged on my ceiling for you the other time he ran amok, but you were out, and I had to call the cops.' She reaches out to touch him, but doesn't quite make it. 'Bruiser, just walk with me downstairs. I'm late.'

'Hang on, let me showyer something, only take a second.'

He flings open his cupboard to a dazzle of perfectly ironed shirts, hanging in impeccable rows. 'Whaddyer reckon?'

He caresses an ornate cuff. 'Go on, have a feel.'

She touches the silk. He knows he's untouchable, but not the shirts.

'Lovely, Bruiser. You'll kill them in that. But there's a raving lunatic downstairs waiting to demolish me with his lethal carpet-sweeper. And I'm late for work.'

'Won't hurt you, sweetie. Just a bit sick,' he says, sadly putting his precious shirts on the sofa and escorting her downstairs.

Seeing Bruiser at her side, the man downstairs retreats. But not before Bruiser nods to him, embarrassed.

'Takes all sorts,' he murmurs, wishing she'd stay and see his hand-stitching and listen to some records.

TWENTY-THREE

Lillian is at the agent's to complain about the man downstairs. It is women he hates. The two girls in the backyard came to Lillian for refuge. He had knocked on their door, and when it was ajar quickly stuck his foot in the crack, aiming his gun at their heads. Their record-player was too loud; there was too much rock 'n' roll; too many young men; too much laughter.

'He not only threatened me, he drew a gun on the girls in the backyard. He trips me up with his carpet-sweeper every time I go out. He kicks the girls' dog.'

'Dogs aren't allowed on the premises. It's in the contract. Dirty, dangerous animals.'

'It's the man who's dirty and dangerous, actually.'

The agent's face reddens, incensed by the patronizing emphasis.

'What do you expect, *actually*? If you choose to live alone you get what's coming to you.'

'I beg your pardon?'

'You heard. You women. You shouldn't be living on your own. What have you done with your husband? Don't come whining to me for protection. You want it both ways.'

It's useless. She stalks out and tries to regain her equilibrium by staring in the window of the pavlova shop. On white cliffs of meringue and cream, strawberries and passion-fruit glimmer enticingly.

She marches into the hotel for a drink and takes it to the window-seat. The men eye her. Then look away. She is neither young nor old, neither pretty nor ugly, neither smart nor arty. A hybrid.

A young father, his belly pregnant with beer, carries his son on his shoulders. He waves to the crocodile of inmates from the Far West Home, now trooping back in their red cardigans to tea. But none of them waves back.

The sea is so churned up after another storm that they have had to close the beach. The waves send a fine spray so high in the sky it could be mist. Hysterical gulls conglomerate on the sand, picking over the washed-up litter from the yachts, piercing the bluebottles, then veer up in white windy arcs when a dog, which is breaking the law by being on the beach, pelts towards them, barking.

Simon arrives late tonight. The sitting-room is a dismal windowless alcove, so they always use the bedroom which leads to the balcony, the sea, the gulls, the ships, the glamour of the Milky Way.

But tonight they must shut it all out. Because rain is flying in. They are cooped up together.

He slumps in the only chair with his coat collar up, glinting with raindrops, holding his inevitable flagon of Riesling. Lillian reclines on the bed with a cigarette, wondering why he hasn't taken off his coat, given her one of his huge, disarming smiles.

Their secret romance has been going on for weeks. She is starting to relax; secure enough to feel a slow-burning content. Her face is filling out, changing. The peaky look has gone.

The pleasure she feels at the prospect of his nightly visitations (his angelic descents) she keeps carefully under lock and key. She does not take him seriously, or tell him things.

But being with him, apart from all the world, in their little room by the sea, has a timeless interplanetary feeling.

'Shall we put on the new Dylan record?' she asks.

'I can't stand Dylan.'

She looks at him with surprise. How uncomfortable he seems, hunched there, in his raincoat. Sulky, almost.

A quiet, cold contraction starts in her belly. 'You choose one then. And pour us a drink. Maybe there's a play or an old movie on TV.'

'Let's go out.'

'Out?'

'Yes, for God's sake, let's go somewhere. We always stay in. Why don't we go out?'

He turns his head backwards and forwards like an asthmatic struggling for breath.

'You know why.'

'You're so fucking conventional.'

'Anyway, we've got no money.'

'Look, let's go for a walk, at least, for half an hour. To get some fresh air.'

Lillian rises from her bower and leads the way through the cluttered hall where her coat is hanging. He follows, still clutching the wrapped flagon. A bad sign, that.

They walk stiffly side by side in the wind to the opposite bay. Yes, he is getting bored. Stifled. She has seen that caged, sulky look on the faces of boys before.

'Is that schoolteacher still pursuing you in his yellow jeep?'

'Oh *him*. He's all right.'

'Good God. *The Baragoola* is out. The ferries must be running after all. I was sure they'd cancelled them today because of the storm.'

'They go out in almost any conditions. Anyway.' He sniffs the wind. 'It's easing up.'

'Look, the pier is open. Whoopee! Who'd have thought it.' He cheers up. Does a little caper near the famous slogan: *Manly Fun Pier: Seven Miles From Sydney and a Thousand Miles from Care.*

But inside it is empty of patrons. The attendant is just locking the gates of the dodgems.

'The Octopus and Ferris Wheel are still open. But put on your hood. Don't want earache do we?'

'I haven't been up in that wheel since . . .' she hesitates, not wanting to mention the exact date.

'Oh all right. I'm coming. I'll indulge you, beautiful lady.' His smile is loose and shimmering. He screws the top back on the flagon. 'Don't worry babe, you'll have a swig when we're flying high.'

The man takes money from her while Simon looks away, climbing ahead into the carriage. They shoot skywards. The man waits below, looking dully at the spangled cliffs. You can get used to anything.

The Harbour and its bobbing boats shrink. The tide-line of seaweed and bluebottles stretches from cliff to cliff. Each time the ferry rocks in the distance between The Heads, it disappears under a wave. Rain feathers their faces.

'How about a swig?' she asks.

With conspiratorial charm he takes off the top and hands her the flagon. A whiplash of wind sends the carriage teetering, and the glass hits her teeth; sour wine drops on her coat.

'Christ! The ferry's rocking. I thought it was going to sink, just then. I wouldn't like to be crossing The Heads in it now. They'll be wading in water,' she says.

'It's fun then. All the old Mums scream and drag their kids away from the railings.'

'I'm an old Mum,' she reminds him, coldly.

He stares at her. 'You're mad to worry about going out with me. It doesn't matter what people think. I don't care. I love you. Strange woman.'

'I love you, too,' she says, sadly, lightly.

'What's the problem then? Job eating you? If it is, leave it.'

'Oh, you know, some jobs are easy. Others . . .' The Ananda Marga story has been turned down again.

'Let's go to dinner. There's a joint I know in The Cross. We'll do the town. You can flaunt me. I'm proud of you. You should be proud of me.'

'We haven't got any money.' What a repressed, old-fashioned hypocrite she was.

'Well, let's drive south. I can borrow Dad's car. It's full of petrol.'

They drive south, her and the boy, in his father's car, to his father's block of land on a windswept beach. It rains for three days, so they stay in the hut. She reads his father's paperback books and drinks his father's wine. They make love five times, and she imagines it is his father, while the rain pings on the roof like chestnuts.

They get tired of waiting for it to dry and run over the scrub on to the sodden beach, watched through binoculars by an amazed resident from his cliff-top verandah. She has stopped being ashamed of her body. It's not so bad. Gulls scavenge the shore. A lone fisherman near the reef pulls in a fish every time he throws his line. Pollution hasn't reached this southern sea.

The current sweeps her from the centre to the reef in less than a minute. Sharks lurk under these rocks. She looks down at her limbs, juicy morsels.

'Let's go into town, Simon.'

They drive in and find a fish restaurant on a jetty. It's completely empty. It's out of season. The waitress takes their order and disappears for what seems like hours. They sit opposite each other, a mistake. Then turn to stare at the boats on the calm water, counting the barnacles on their hulls.

The comfortable silence has been going on long enough. Lies of omission. Repressed truths push at the seams of their silence.

Bernard telephones from London: 'Listen *ma belle*. It's no good writing to me about money. You are evading your responsibilities. When are you going to come to your senses?'

'I had no alternative, Bernard.'

'What's that supposed to mean?'

'I would have died if I'd stayed in that atmosphere. At least the boys haven't got a corpse for a mother.'

'What about their feelings? My God, my mother was right about you. It takes one bitch to recognize another.'

'I didn't plan it this way. It's *you* who withheld love. For years, Bernard, *years*. At any time you could have reached over to me and said, "Let's talk about this." But you didn't and you wouldn't let me.'

'You're obviously suffering from menopausal madness.' How controlled his voice sounds. Nothing flamboyant, even now.

'You've been calling me menopausal for ten years. I think you mean menstrual. Either way, how can a natural condition be used as a term of abuse?'

They are two wolves tearing over scraps, on a desolate plain.

Her next job is to interview the famous Australian writer, Alf Rutter. She is given an address which conveniently turns out to be in Manly. But on the hilly side. She climbs the steps of a modern block. A woman opens the door. 'I'm Tessa. Don't worry. Alf knows you're coming. He'll turn up. But . . .' Tessa gives a bubbling laugh, 'he's not the most reliable man.'

Lillian is led into a beautiful, octagonal room. Chips of the Harbour flash through every window.

Tessa has a white Persian kitten which chases Lillian's pen every time she makes a note. She is determined to get this article accepted. 'Tell me, does Alf Rutter stay with you every time he comes to Sydney?'

'Mostly. We're old, old mates.'

On the wall there's a mural consisting of a man's trousered legs. It's a child's view of the patriarch permanently striding into the room laden with presents and fabulous news.

'Alf's just been to Paris for the first time in his life. He waited until he was sixty. Now he thinks everything uttered in a foreign accent is somehow deeper and more meaningful and definitely more erotic.'

'I went to Paris soon after I arrived in London. In the hotel on the Left Bank I met a Dutchman who said, "When you are young and when you are beeyooteefull . . . eet ees good too looove." And it thrilled me to the marrow. I thought it was the most profound remark anyone had ever made.'

Tessa puts her glass down suddenly. Her face askew, like a hugged and battered rag doll. 'I'm pregnant. I'm going to have an abortion tomorrow.'

Lillian flexes her fingers slowly, then thoughtfully pings the edges of the Venetian glass. 'How old are you?'

'Thirty-eight.'

'Ever had children?'

'Nope.'

'Who's the father?'

'Doesn't matter. A ship in the night. I'll have to have an abortion.'

'You've obviously got money. Do you own this flat?'

'Yes. Isn't it nice? Have you noticed you can see the Harbour from all six windows. That's what I like about Sydney Harbour, all the wriggly bits. It's like an octopus.'

'You could turn that study into a fine baby's room. You're mad if you don't have it.'

'I'm mad if I do.' Tessa scoops up the glasses and hurries away into the kitchen. She's one of those women who can fix up a meal in a few minutes that tastes as if she's been working on it for days.

'I've got a lousy job as it is, designing crap for a factory. What could I do with a kid weighing me down? The world is full of thirty-eight-year-old women who've had a thousand affairs, panicking, trying to get pregnant before it's too late. Or haven't you noticed. The *desperate* thirty-eighters. They suddenly see the long shadows ahead. They're paying the lonely price for all that sixties fucking around. It's a baby or a breakdown.'

'Men say women earth them. They say a woman is their earth-wire. That's why politicians who live among lies have so many mistresses. Well, men don't earth *us*, Tessa. Babies do. All men do for you if you fancy them is make you long for more. Passion resonates under a woman's skin for longer. I'm convinced of that. A baby calms you. Connects you to the past and to the future . . .' The doctor who prevented her abortion had been more succinct.

BALLADE OF THE DEAD
LADIES

TWENTY-FOUR

She stood, rubbing the small of her back, amid cases, crates, wrinkled-up newspapers. Light from the street-lamp sawed the room in half. The curtains weren't up yet. Her back ached.

She couldn't remember in which crate she'd packed the sheets. Then she saw one with white fabric peeking through the cracks. But it was Bernard's tropical suit.

She held it up. Aha, another love-note from the air hostess. She considered putting it back in his breast pocket, sending the suit off to the laundry. But she didn't feel jealous enough.

She screwed it up and tossed it among the rest of the debris.

She stared at herself in the mirror over the fireplace. She looked excited. There was something good about moving.

The doorbell rang, making her start, caught in an act of vanity.

Through the curtainless window she saw Robert, without Felicity. He was holding something black and squirming.

When she let him in, the cat jumped on the carpetless floor, and paused, gauging the splinters, and obstacles.

'Come in, Robert. How lovely to see you.' Her voice echoed. Their footsteps banged loudly on the wooden slats. 'You're my first visitor in the new house. Bernard's in Provence at a big auction. But I've got some duty-free Scotch.'

'Water.' He slumped on a crate. She had an urge to pummel him back into shape. He was such a blob. The cat walked about with its tail curled up. Astounded.

'I've been trying and trying to phone you.'

'Oh Robert. We're not on the phone yet. The move to London has been horrific. All that gear we'd collected!'

Robert moved his head from side to side. In his silence the cat had time to approach Lillian; she felt honoured.

'The boys have gone off to a dance-hall in Camden Lock to celebrate their escape from the Lycees.' How prim they had looked in their neat French haircuts.

The clock on the floor ticked, and each tick echoed and resonated on the splintery floor.

'Why didn't Felicity come with you?'

'Look, I'm on my way to Ireland. I'm taking the children to live in County Kerry. I want you to have the cat. Felicity said you were fond of the cat.'

Lillian gazed at him. The trouble with being abroad is that things happen to your friends and you can't keep up. You are always the last to hear the news.

'I'm happy to mind the cat. When will you be back? Felicity can't live without it.'

'Oh, never I hope. I'm selling the house.'

The house in which she had so often sat with Felicity, where the petunias and camellias had bloomed so faithfully every year.

'We're not really a family any more. Felicity dead. The children nearly grown-up.'

The cat sprang on Lillian's lap and twirled round and round, looking desperately for a comfortable spot. He started kneading her, his claws tearing her thighs through the denim.

Lillian doubled up, almost asphyxiating the cat. '*Dead*?'

'It happened ten days ago. The funeral is over. I couldn't get hold of you . . . I thought some . . . '

Robert paused. His mouth moved soundlessly like a fish's.

The clock hammered.

'No one told me. I didn't know.'

She noticed her arms were trembling, and she was glad when the cat scratched her.

'Pills and booze she used. A fatal combi . . . '

They both waited. She held vigil over his silence.

' . . . nation.'

Lillian got up off the packing case. Her leg cracked. She walked towards Robert. People, she knew, fornicated in the ruins of earthquakes. She understood why. She touched Robert's shoulder noticing her confident seducer's fingers.

'But *why*?' she moaned.

He groped in his pocket and produced an old letter. He handed it to her as if it was a boulder. The stamp was, as she expected, Nigerian. She opened it with difficulty and read a proposal of marriage from Josh.

'No, it can't be that. I gave it to her years ago, in your garden. It was stuck under the lino in our old flat by that nutty janitor.'

She gulped a glass of whisky, a fire-bomb in her belly.

'She used to get . . . you know . . . de . . . '

'pressed,' finished Lillian. 'Depressed.'

'I gave her pills for it. I shouldn't have. I see that now. But they seemed to work. I thought, It'll pass. It's her age.'

'Everyone gets depressed. You can't not. The way things are.'

She was rocking Robert in her arms. Perhaps her children had disappointed her. They always did one way or another. 'She was *fragile*, Lillian. More than we knew.'

You didn't want to be the world's greatest artist, like Katherine.
You didn't want to be the world's greatest lover, like Sonia.
You wanted to jog along, get by, be nice. You were the mistress of compromise.
And yet you cracked. I wish I had been on hand for you that day, Felicity, as you were always on hand for me. You sat on the edge of my bed at World's End combing out all the knots in my hair. It took you three hours. My hair was as matted as a mad woman's.

Lillian picked the rotting flowers off the wreath. Yes, friendship, the real thing, just grows. You don't have to cultivate it.

Alarm bells were going off in house after house all over London. It was as if the empty houses were wailing. The cries of the little burglar alarms fixed on the front walls were completely ignored, like the cries of babies in a busy hospital.

Lillian had woken up at four. Unable to sleep. Had scribbled a postcard to Lucan, care of the Archaeological Institute.

She put the card in the letterbox, moist with morning dew. The world is full of such fragile, tentative feelers.

Now, above her, the last star flickered out. It could be a galaxy. Another entire system of sun, moons, planets, all whirling in their various temperatures and magnitudes.

She went into a café and bought a cup of tea. Two labourers were reading yesterday's *Daily Mirror*. Felicity should have gone out more. They should have met in secret, like lovers, her and Felicity, to discuss the universe.

The day they met in St Paul's, Felicity had been standing in the main aisle with a guidebook. Lillian stopped crying. On such ordinary things tremendous structures are built.

Felicity had rescued her, had taken her back to World's End and said, 'You can share this with me.'

Felicity could iron sheets and fold them end-to-end perfectly. Lillian could throw open cupboard doors and confront rotting meat-loaves, mouldy bread, disposing of them without fuss. Basically, they were compatible.

But Felicity always left the soap to go slimy at the bottom of the bath, and Lillian never closed the top of the cereal packet. And there was one important thing they didn't share. Something Felicity had shared with Sonia; Sonia had shared with Katherine . . .

All those dead ladies.

TWENTY-FIVE

Night after night there was only Bernard and her. His pinched face. His little incisors masticating the food. Did he count the chews? Forty-eight times for each mouthful, as his mother had insisted? The boys were always out.

'They're not studying at all, Bernard. I could try torturing them. But it's too much fun here. London's a ball for kids their age.'

Bernard shrugged. 'It's your job to bring up the children. It's mine to make money. I do my job. Why can't you do yours? You know I have to travel constantly.' He reached over for some trout, spooning out the cheeks. She felt her cheeks shrivel.

The unhappiness between them was no longer concealed by the endless fuss of motherhood. Perhaps Bernard didn't feel the chill, the endless oddity of their estrangement. *Not even talking about it*! Perhaps he had nothing better to compare it with. His mother's house at Neuilly creaking with resentments. Perhaps he saw it as the norm. He wished to re-create it. Isn't that what they said?

But she'd been raised in a house on a headland, full of the sound of slamming doors and visitors. Quarrels and reconciliations. Playing with a toy on the kitchen steps, she'd looked up and seen her father kissing her mother. They were swaying together as if pushed by some invisible wind, although the curtains didn't flutter. She felt reassured, terribly happy.

But when her mother was alone, on hot, dusty afternoons, without visitors, she would complain. 'I shouldn't have married your father. I should have travelled . . .' Lillian could feel her yearning as her own. Lillian had done her mother's travelling for her.

Angus had rung up to invite himself for lunch.

'Bernard away, I suppose. I'll bring a bottle of champagne,' he said, and she knew what he had in mind.

They met with that curious mixture of excitement and lack of future that exists between old lovers. He was wearing a hat. She laughed outright. He tossed it across the room. The lover's hat.

'Better not let me forget that. Don't want to leave any clues do we?' He handed her the bottle with a little bow. 'Your husband's in France. He would expect you to take a lover in the afternoon.'

'As long as I don't talk about it.'

'I remember you always used to say, "We must be candid. If we could tell each other the truth, everything would be all right."'

'What an idiot I was.'

He was prowling round the room, checking the exits. 'You always used to say, "Men should have fire. Women should be

143

beautiful." But I wasn't firey enough for you. You needed a whole team of us.'

'And I wasn't smart enough for you.'

'How are the boys?'

'Manic. Adolescence I suppose. Dressing oddly. Always out. Dropping all their studies. The eldest is always angry with me.' She didn't want to talk about it. Perhaps he was angry with her for having made a lousy choice, out of fatigue and convention.

She had set the table with flowers in the centre, like a seduction scene in a film.

He smiled, and the champagne cork hit the ceiling. He admired the fireplace, the chairs, the pale, brocade curtains. 'I couldn't fall in love with you before, somehow. Not quite. But I think I could now.'

She smiled bitterly. The new elegance of her surroundings reflected an inner capability and commonsense that he admired in a woman. But he must be joking. She had seen his diary; seen her name crammed in between a dozen appointments.

'Do you run into Lucan?' she inquired over lunch.

'He's abroad most of the time. Doubtless in a pit, scraping some seven thousand-year-old antiquity.'

'I suppose he avoids women now.'

Angus lit a cigarette, flinching from the extravagant flame. 'He's married again, I hear.'

Lillian sighed. 'Well, I hope she's a survivor.'

'Come here. Stop talking. You're still beautiful.'

She pulled the curtains and put the chain on the front door, in case the boys came skipping back. The fire crackled pleasantly.

He stubbed out his black cigarette and undressed her on the rug that Bernard had brought back from South America.

The vein in his forehead stood out. Now that he had lost more hair she saw how it continued over his scalp, making him oddly vulnerable. He had always been so competent. So busy.

Afterwards, dressing, she talked a lot, trying to drown her

144

sense of bleakness; the sad implication of her willingness to fuck for old time's sake.

'How are the books going, Angus? Still churning 'em out?'

'Business is booming. I'm even giving lecture tours in the States.'

'What do you lecture on? How to get rich quick in publishing?'

Angus picked up the empty champagne bottle and walked into the kitchen to hide it in the bin. Adultery for him was a way of life. With his back to her he said, 'The stories of Katherine Feldmann. She has a fatal effect on those little American college kids. The ones who love to seduce their professors.'

'I see. I see.' She gazed at him, wanting to talk about it.

Angus lit a cigarette with the same old lighter, flinching from its huge flame.

'One day you'll burn your beard off.'

'I'm thinking of shaving it. What do you think? Perhaps growing it was a mistake. It's half-grey, anyhow.'

'Most men grow beards to hide weak chins. but yours is too strong. Leave it on.'

'It must have been frightful for you when Felicity killed herself,' he ventured at last.

'Robert gave her tablets for depression. I've tried to tell myself it might have been an accident. He warned her not to mix them with booze, but you know how forgetful she was.'

'Come off it, Lillian. She was never vague enough to poison those spoiled children of hers. So why this?'

'We always believed she was the strong one. The sane one. It was convenient to believe that. She was close to Sonia though.'

'That evil bitch.' The bones ridged in his normally bland face.

'Come on, Angus. She was just crazy about Lucan. Women kill for less.'

'Didn't give a fuck about anyone else.'

'She wasn't what you'd call *sympathetic*.'

'I was never much bothered about why she killed herself. I saw it somehow as another malignant act on her part. But Felicity. I remember her as such a sweet, sensible person. You can never tell . . .'

Lillian remained unusually silent.

He leaned back and studied her. That beautiful hair was losing its sheen.

'Oh all right. Lost love and all that. Bitter regrets. But she had that nice husband of hers, doctor whatsisname, and she had children. *Children*! They'll never get over it. They'll always think she didn't love them enough to live.'

It wasn't that. It was simply that the call when it came was irresistible. To put a stop to all the pain. He must see that.

She spoke at last. 'When Sonia did it, after Katherine Feldmann, I think it might have presented itself as a viable option.'

Angus was frowning at her. His face made of some harder substance now.

'Don't worry about my following suit. I'll break the chain. I'm too "up myself", as the Australians say, to kill myself.'

'You need a Christmas holiday in Sydney. Just lie in the sun and forget this gloomy place.'

'It's the one real decision we can make every day of our lives. Camus knew it . . .'

'Balls.' Angus screwed down his cigarette in the ashtray. 'A survivor if ever I saw one. You'll be a leathery old lady.'

He reminded her of the time they spent Christmas together on the cross-channel ferry, and groaned ritualistically at the prospect of Christmas festivities.

'Ours will be taken care of by relatives. Boiling turkey under a boiling sun. I'm amazed Bernard wants to join me again this year. It's his French reverence for the family.'

'Are you taking the boys?'

146

'No. They want to stay here with their girls.'

His eyes moved restlessly around the room. To him, she had already gone.

'I'll send you a postcard.'

They pecked each other goodbye. She stood at the door and saw him wait for the traffic lights to change and cross the highway. She saw a small, forceful, gingerish man, hurrying home with his dog, leaving his favourite old flame to get on with her life.

ABSOLUTION AND AFTER

TWENTY-SIX

Lillian sweeps the balcony, driving the lopsided broom in energetic arcs from wall to balustrade; shoving over browning pine-needles, parrot feathers and sand-droppings from the surfboard which has now been huffily removed.

She has moved all the furniture about, in an ecstasy of change, putting the sofa where the table was, and the table in the alcove; underneath she had found encrustations which she scraped, swept, washed.

Out goes a burst balloon and a shower of dust before her broom. This gorgeous feeling is not to do with her monthly hormonal oscillations but the jubilation of an honourable freedom.

It is all over with Simon. She has cut the cord. She will miss him; all too soon; feel lonely. He drove her away from her house so fast he crashed into a fence on a hairpin bend. Now there's a big gap where the fence had been, on the main bus route into the city.

The triumph she feels is over herself; the craven, clutching part.

The sky is its usual relentless blue. The first cars are manoeuvring for parking space, and the megaphone has already made its daily pronouncement. Now the megaphone crackles again:

'A glass eye has been found on the beach. Anyone who has lost the er-object can claim it at the Surf Club. And (crackle, crackle) will mothers warn their children about the bluebottles.'

Lillian moves an iron stretcher and exposes a rusty piece of meccano, a fungoid apple-core, an old condom. She sends these relics from other ghostly tenants flying over the balcony. Then remembers, too late, that there might be a passer-by getting clobbered below. She looks over apprehensively and sees the Bad Man on a deck chair below. He leaps up, brushing grit off his balding dome.

'That does it!' His face is swollen and lumpy like a toad's. Beyond his blotched head the sea glitters, appealing to him to take a larger view.

'Sorry about that.'

'Sorry. You'll be sorry. I'm going to the agent to inform them about the goings-on at your place.'

'Goings-on?'

He gives her a menacing, contemptuous cackle.

'You know you're very dirty-minded. Do you know that?'

'Oh shut up.' He backs off and adopts an embattled stance. 'It's you or me in this house. And it'll be you who goes. You won't like that now, will you? Then where will you go?' He gives her an evil smile.

She stares at him. He thinks this dump is all she has in the world. She looks out at the shining cliffs to where the reef re-directs the sea. She wouldn't like to be thrown out, blast his eyes.

She is giving a dinner party. It has always seemed ridiculous to entertain in this tiny place. But Angus has telephoned from London to announce his imminent arrival in Sydney for a two-day conference with his Australian distributors. She knows that he will enjoy her beach hut.

Merla in the shop is crying again. 'What's up, Merla?'

'He counts the grapes whenever he comes back, in case I've eaten any.'

'You should go out more.'

'He won't let me go out. I'm thirty-one.'

'Help me carry all this food upstairs, will you. I'll make you a coffee. He can't object to that.'

Merla's black eyes flick agreement. She goes into the back of the shop and emerges with her husband, his belly drooping over his shorts.

'I'll carry it up for you,' he says, pre-empting their dangerous plot.

But as he thumps ahead of her upstairs Lillian says loudly, 'Your wife should go out more. She seems rather sad. Alienated.'

'Alie-whated? Jeez. You've swallowed the dictionary.' He puts down the box. 'And that's why I chose a Filipino wife. They don't shout at you and boss you around. They're trained to please men.' He gave a lewd cackle.

Yes. They bring in the coffee on all fours, carrying it on their backs. They keep quiet for years, but they disintegrate early. She turns her back on him, making elaborate business with her keys.

He shouts back from the landing, 'If she ever gets too sad I say, "Right, love, I'll send you back to the slums of Manila." That shuts her up.'

Lillian goes on to the balcony and yells at the sea-view.

'That's why she married you, you prick, to get away from all that degradation.' But it was going to be hard for him to keep Merla cooped up in Manly where every day she saw free women walking about in bikinis and sarongs. One day some boy in thongs would just reach over the counter and scoop her up. Merla should continue to cry ostentatiously at her customers.

The priest from the seminary on the hill is the first to arrive. An affable man, his Catholicism, which is as endemic to him as his Irishness, does not seem to interest him so much as literature. He never comes to any social occasion without plastic bags full of books and booze.

He is embarrassed to find that he is the first arrival, but Lillian puts him on the balcony which is all lit by candles. As usual, he travels in disguise, in ordinary unpriestly garb. But like a girl wearing mini-skirts on a train, he is perversely afraid that someone might try to pick him up. He piles up a protective wall of plastic bags.

He draws out his first can of beer and gazes at it tenderly. 'I've brought my own.' She met the priest at the office pub where he mixes with the journalists. She suspects him of spying on the ungodly.

'So the great Angus is in our midst. I didn't hear the earth shake! What's he doing in this part of the world? Extending his empire?'

The jazz-singer arrives wearing a Balinese sarong and frangipanis in her auburn hair. The priest gazes out to sea.

As usual, the singer has a battered, speechless look as if there is too much to communicate and words will not suffice. But, after a huge whisky, she sits humming at the sea, its amniotic beat soothing her. She flicks her fingers through the candle flames to see how slowly she can do it before it hurts, only breaking off to ask about the man downstairs.

When Angus arrives, the priest stands up in delight.

'You've done it again Lillian! It must be like being on permanent holiday.' He is stunned by the imminence of the sea.

Inevitably, the name of Katherine Feldmann comes up and her seminal *Collected Works*.

The female wail in it makes the priest weary and wary. Its despair is unacceptable. Suicide is a mistake. Like sewing on the wrong button. It embarrasses him. But mention of sex does not.

'You'll have to see our topless beach before you depart these shores. It's just below the seminary. Makes a great training-ground for our young priests.'

Angus tells him how in California the students at his lectures were always claiming that Katherine Feldmann's stories were allegories about menstruation. The priest laughs.

When Lillian goes into the kitchen to make coffee, scraping oyster and prawn shells into the bin, she feels the relief of a hostess who has created something diverting.

Angus joins her in the kitchen. He leans against the table. His eyes dancing. 'You said something on the phone about a midnight swim.'

'Oh!' She straightens up, remembers his old, hustling ways, brushes past him and joins the others on the balcony.

'We're going for a midnight swim. Want to join us anyone?'

No, they don't want to move. The priest feels threatened no longer. He wants to listen to the singer then get her on to some Irish ditties.

She is cradling her guitar as if it is a baby and is singing softly:

Life begins to show
Round midnight, midnight . . .

The two old friends walk out of the house carrying towels. They do what she has always wanted to do but was too frightened of prowlers to attempt alone. They are walking along Fairy Bower at night towards the rock-pool.

On a bench a man in make-up is scorching passers-by with his eyes. The hoot of the last Manly ferry wails over the rocks. A stray dog forages under a rock for rotting fish.

At the pool, all is quiet. She takes off her sarong and jumps in, clothed by darkness. On boiling nights like this just to walk down perfumed streets listening to music scatter from Sydney windows can make her swallow with excitement. She dives into the still, black pool, breaking up the reflection of the Milky Way.

She hears the clean splash of Angus diving. A midnight swim at last.

In the water Angus waits patiently for some love. A businessman needs his consolation.

When she comes close enough, they kiss. And kiss. She wraps her legs around him, buoyed up by the water. The coldness of the sea is the strongest sensation. It is not a particularly sexual act, but they continue their ritual. Its power is symbolic, a sealing of some ancient pact, reminding him he is human, and her that she is not alone.

Two men, not the men Sydney women are searching for, but the others, the ones who actually inhabit the land, lurch by on their way home from the Steyne Hotel, holding each other up as they push each other down, boxing the air in retaliation. They stare at the black silhouettes of Angus and Lillian, now decently separated. They want to join the party.

They lean over, swaying, like children reaching for balloons, nearly hurting their heads on slippery rocks, and roll up their trousers.

Holding bottles aloft in the air like rescuers, they wade in.

Angus and Lillian stay put on the far side of the pool.

'Have you got a boyfriend here?' Angus asks, treading water.

'Give us a kiss, darling,' comes a yell.

'No, not really.'

'What is that supposed to mean?'

'Mean cow!' comes a bellow ... subsiding into a giggle.

'I meet men at work. But nothing seems to happen. I've got a funny manner and I'm getting old.'

She floats on her back, hoisting her legs and pushing out against the sides of the pool, jetting in one swift movement almost to the other. Her face is smoothed by starlight and the recent reminder of her body's core.

'You're just switched off. After that cold computer you married. You don't trust men. And they pick that up.'

'Fuck you then, you stuck-up wankers,' comes a shout. But the abuse has no menace in it.

'Angus?'

'Hmmmm?' He dog-paddles up to her while the drunks cat-call, guffaw, roister in the shallows.

'Okay. Lillian. What's up? *'Open thy dark saying upon the harp and I shall incline mine ear to a parable.'* I read that in a framed bible today on your Central Station. There are so many fundamentalists about.'

'They're called *wowsers*.'

'Well, what do you want to tell me?'

'You remember, oh years ago, in London, you gave me Katherine Feldmann's telephone number?'

'Did I?' He stops agitating the water. The waves twist beside him in their most secret crevices. A night-crab scuttles.

'You were doing your tycoon thing and trying to fix me up with another job because I was bored selling books.'

'So?'

'I made an appointment to see her at nine on the morning she died. I did intend to go. But I didn't turn up. I *didn't turn up!*'

Angus is momentarily baffled. He feels waterlogged, chilly.

She must make it clear. So he can absolve her.

'She had given me meticulous instructions on the phone. I

was to let myself in if she didn't hear the bell. It was faulty. She left it for me under the mat. But I didn't turn up. She knew I was coming.'

A bottle breaks on the rocks. There will be broken glass in the morning, always a hateful sight. But those murderous edges, after a certain time, become completely smoothed out, made benign by erosion.

'I was meant to save her life.'

She cries properly at last. Salt tears mix with salt sea.

'Christ, Lillian.' The vein in his forehead throbs.

'You don't believe in Christ.'

'Ah, hell, then.' One of the drunks drops his trousers and waggles his bum under the moon. Angus's face sets as if dealing with a massive corporate problem.

'Why didn't you tell me this before? Strictly speaking you should have gone to the inquest.'

'I was guilty and afraid. And I couldn't tell you because you were going out with smarter women. I hated you because you didn't think I was good enough for you.'

'As a matter of interest, why didn't you turn up, Lillian? You're usually so punctual.'

'I meant to. But at the last minute I couldn't face her. I felt too guilty.'

'Guilty?'

'At one of your parties I met Lucan. The minute I met him we rushed off into the night. I followed when he whistled. Out into Hampstead Heath.'

'Ah. That.' Angus dives into the water to clear his head, emerging in one swift coil.

'I hope you're not going to spend your whole life being guilty about an act most women these days do reflexively. Her suicide wasn't your fault, you know.'

'I keep telling myself that.' And Lillian thinks, studying his face, It wasn't your fault either, despite a certain lack of attention to detail.

'I should have been more considerate. We should both have been more considerate.'

'Oh, I did my best. I always promoted her work. Christ, I practically invented her.'

She looks down at the sea.

The wind has dropped, and the drunks ramble off.

Angus looks at her angrily. A rare stillness possesses him. Didn't she know you always feel guilty about the dead.

'I knew about your rushing off into the night with Lucan. It hurt my pride, of course.'

'And Lucan and I haven't even remained friends.'

'At least you survive, darling.' In an almost conscious gesture of absolution he lifts his hand full of water and lets it sprinkle on her head. Baptismal drops.

'Like you, Angus.'

TWENTY-SEVEN

Once in a museum she had seen some stones taken from a crocodile's belly. Now she could digest her own crocodile stone. She dives into the dark, rasping water of home.

TWENTY-SEVEN

Lillian visits Tessa who is very pregnant but raw-eyed from weeping.

'Christ, Tessa, regrets already?'

'Nope. It's not having a baby I'm crying about. It's bloody men.'

Lillian follows her inside, beyond the huge mirror reflecting a colossal fern, dyed silver.

Tessa's rag-doll face looks as if it's been hurled out of a seventh-storey window. She lights a cigarette.

'You shouldn't be smoking so much. Or drinking.' But she cannot forcibly dash the cigarette from her mouth or wrench away the bottle in her hands. She politely accepts a drink.

'Well, what's up?'

'Oh, I went to an art exhibition, an opening. I was standing in the background and up strides the painter Caesar Langley and sweeps me off my feet.'

'It's hard to imagine, with the weight you are now.'

'He thinks pregnant women are beautiful. And I did need some attention. It's bloody lonely with no one to cuddle you and tell you how clever you're being.'

'Sure.'

'We spent a heavenly night. I didn't realize pregnant women could have so much fun. But then he made careful plans to meet me for lunch the next day. He insisted. We were going out on his yacht.'

Lillian pours herself another drink.

'You must have been looking forward to a wonderful lunch,' encourages Lillian.

'The bastard didn't show up. You've guessed already.'

'A lovely, considerate human being.'

'I sat and sat, and the waiters started to whisper.'

'Have you heard from him since?'

'No.'

Lillian springs up and rushes to the phone, demanding this bastard's address.

She dictates a telegram to Caesar Langley: NOT ONLY DO YOU STAND UP A PREGNANT WOMAN THEN YOU PRETEND NOTHING HAS HAPPENED STOP WHAT A LOW SPECIMEN OF HUMANITY YOU ARE GOD IS WATCHING YOU.

When she leaves she holds the banisters carefully with both hands. The concrete floor seems determined to smack her in the face. She has insisted on borrowing Tessa's car to get home. She notes that Alf Rutter is following her.

Once inside the car she rolls down the window to give Alf's gnarled face a goodnight peck. He puts his head in through the window and presses a kiss on her, his hands groping at her dress. She plots to roll up the window and behead him. She can see the headlines: FAMOUS AUTHOR FOUND BE-HEADED IN MANLY.

'I can't breathe, Alf.'

He draws his head away. She presses the accelerator to the

159

floor and hears him shouting abuse as she drives away. She swerves down the hill shouting, 'Raped! Almost raped! And by a bushwhacker. I'll kill him. Kill! Kill! Kill!'

But in the morning she laughs; not scared of men anymore.

But she isn't going to get involved with her boss. He looks at her like someone examining the contents of a dirty fridge.

'Well?'

'Can I interrupt a moment? I've got an idea for a profile.'

The editor puts down his papers with studied reluctance. His wife and assistant, known as 'The Radiant Doormat', is sitting beside him, looking at him with eyes abject with multiple orgasms.

On his other side he has his favourite sycophant.

They stare with dislike. Do they disapprove that she has left her husband, she wonders? To all outside observers he is irreproachable. Or are they jealous of her freedom because she is not on the permanent staff? Is it her face they dislike? Her manner? Probably just her accent.

'It's about the Conchita Newton story.'

The editor groans. This is the best known gang crime in town. And this town is run by gang crime.

'I've got a contact who knows something.' She names him.

'That man has no credibility whatsoever. He's been touting that story about for years.' The editor is snarling.

'He is very brave. He's the only man in town who tried to do some probing after they beat him up.'

The editor shrugs, bored.

'He's also a councillor and a strong union activist. I could do a good profile.' She couldn't shut up.

'No! No! *No!*' The editor stands up and shouts. 'No! Bugger off!'

'You rude prick!' she bellows across the clatter and squalor of the newsroom.

It is her nephew's twenty-first.

They're holding it at the boatshed. They're bringing in a pavlova made in the shape of breasts. With sparklers stuck in them, all lit up. On top of the breasts there's a huge silver dollar-sign formed from the number 21. Everyone cheers and claps.

Lillian leans by a pillar, waving to relatives. Knowing it's a joke. But it is not a joke. His success as a trainee insurance salesman is being beatified.

Simon finds her, and they slump together at a side table, balloons popping on the ceiling like bats. 'I've been overseas,' he says. He looks different. Less angelic. Reality has made inroads.

'Some things you never forget. They're set apart,' she hears herself saying. They smile at each other. 'Remember after we decided to end it ... that fence you drove into ... it's a landmark now. Every time the bus passes those bright new palings I feel very proud.'

He turns to her, still serious. She speaks quickly.

'And how did you earn your living overseas, Simon?'

'Oh. This and that.' He looks away.

TWENTY-EIGHT

Lillian is sitting all in one piece, waiting for the last ferry to Manly. A drunk reels across from the pub where he has been holding vigil with his Dæmons, leaning against the ancient beer advertisement of men in plus-fours playing golf, admired by neat women.

He slumps on the ground before her and hums. They seem to be the only late-night revellers this Saturday night. She's been to the Opera House to a concert.

The ferry is late. It is one minute to midnight. She was bored at the concert. The Brahms violin concerto failed to do its usual magic.

The drunk at her feet looks up at her. He has a doomed romantic crush on the redhead in the black coat.

Last week she heard Billie Holliday's voice unexpectedly on her borrowed radio. She was singing 'You Let Me Down' or was it 'Why Did I Depend on You', and Lillian did an unprecedented thing, she switched it off mid moan. She was sick of it. Grief is all right; but not when it becomes a profession.

Lillian feels different now. Armed and dangerous. After the Opera House she went on to the docks to hear some jazz. Freddie Hubbard might be playing. She drank a vodka or two and gazed into the bowels of the glass the way Sonia used to do. Posing a bit.

She had noticed a man in the club. He stood there in the crowds in his beige coat, drab and patient as a fisherman reeling out his line. She was drawn by his secretive, peculiar power.

Out of the dark the incoming ferry appears. Ropes are thrown over bollards; gangplanks thud. Now they open the cage-doors. She hopes there aren't any howling babies on the ferry tonight and thinks of Tessa's new baby, born too small and nervy, but a beauty.

A sudden gust of last-minute passengers clatters up the gangplank. Lillian chooses to sit outside. It's a balmy night. She stares at the silhouettes of the trees in the Botanical Gardens.

Winking yellow lights from the headlands, the red one on top of the bridge, the green one from the lighthouse, scuffle their reflections in the changing sea. In patches of oil they are rainbows. An Italian fishing dinghy veers too close, and the ferry-horn hoots a warning. Gulls circle the fishing-nets, a white ring of greed.

Perhaps she should go back soon; see about the boys; confront Bernard; the house; try to find Felicity's children, and poor Robert.

People prowl up and down feeling the excitement now of crossing The Heads, the Harbour entrance, the open sea.

'Hey! You're not going to do anything silly areyer, sitting out here all alone?'

Why was it so hard to be rooted in the world?

'You're not gonna areyer, sweetie?'

There stands her spiritual guide, still worrying about her, smart as a tailor's dummy, except for his huge, old, tattooed hands and his big, ruined face.

'No. Bruiser. I'm not the type.'

'Where you been then?'

'To the Opera House. And a jazz club on the docks.'

'You never come to listen to me music. Or let me showyer me best tattoo.' It was their old joke.

'I will. I will. And then watch out!'

They are leaning companionably over the rail watching The Heads . . . the Harbour entrance . . . its great hinge always agape. Tempting to some who are born lucky enough to risk going through them, but to others, like Bruiser, offering no temptation.

'Look, I been talkin' to that fella over there, see. I told him I knew yer. He'd like to meetcher.' Bruiser winks. 'Whannim?'

She looks across at some man through the ferry window, over the rows of fake-leather seats where the rip has been sewn up in big cobbled stitches.

A drunk is weaving up the steps. Every time the ship rolls, he sits with a thud.

There is no sea-mist tonight. Each star shines down as bright as Venus, Venus as bright as the moon.

'That's the bloke, over there. Your type. Cultured. He won a few bob on the quinella this arvo. Use to see him sometimes at the arty hotels.' He eyes her wistfully, not understanding why she won't accept him, after all the work he's done on himself.

'Well, make up your mind, sweetie. Areyer comin' or not?'

She stands up. She has waited too long on the shore.

'All right Bruiser. I'm coming.' She gets up and walks, stumbling occasionally, into the rocking ferry.

MORE ABOUT PENGUINS AND PELICANS

West Block

Sara Dowse

Canberra's attendant lords look like settling down after a crisis that has rocked Australia.

In West Block, the flawed human world behind the headlines, George Harland consummates his career as a public servant; Henry Beeker prepares to fight for a policy; Catherine Duffy confronts the consequences of Australia's Vietnam policy; Jonathan Roe stumbles on happiness; and Cassie Armstrong's ironic intelligence leads her to despair.

But the whispers of a different past move through the rumbling hulk of a building which embodies the history of a capital city and has a future as uncertain as the nation it symbolizes.

'West Block celebrates the beauty of an unpopular city, and, with wry wisdom, the human impulses of an often unknown, much disparaged group of people.

Sara Dowse writes with exquisite delicacy, sensing behind her public servants' walls vulnerable inner lives.'

Blanche d'Alpuget

Mr Scobie's Riddle

Elizabeth Jolley

Mr Scobie's arrival at the nursing home of St Christopher and St Jude — and into the clutches of Matron Hyacinth Price — is accidental. Self-educated and still preserving the gift of idyllic memory and wish, Mr Scobie stands apart from the others. For long-term resident and eccentric, Miss Hailey, he represents a kindred spirit; for Matron Price — a lady of questionable practices — the latest victim . . .

But unwittingly Mr Scobie has some recourse — his very simple riddle. Its answer — an ancient commonplace — jolts Matron Price.

Yet it is Mr Scobie's nephew, Hartley, and the group of nocturnal poker players, who ultimately change Matron Price's establishment . . .

'startlingly good . . . it divines riddles of mortality'
Helen Daniel, Melbourne *Age*

'Her writing is splendid, her characters various, her humour delicious.'

Nancy Keesing

'*Mr Scobie's Riddle* is unquestionably Jolley's finest achievement.'

Laurie Clancy

Turtle Beach

Blanche d'Alpuget

'In Blanche d'Alpuget we have a novelist of wit and high intelligence ...'

Christopher Koch,
Sydney Morning Herald

Judith Wilkes, an ambitious journalist, goes to Malaysia to report on an international refugee crisis. Ten years before, Malaysia had provided Judith with her first major career success ... but also with personal disaster.

Through her encounters with Minou, exotic, young French-Vietnamese wife of a high-ranking diplomat, the ambitious Ralph Hamilton, and, ultimately, with enigmatic Kanan who tries to liberate her, Judith is thrown into dramatic personal and professional conflicts.

The train of events have a Graham Greene sense of inevitability as the characters move between cultures and the tensions heighten.

It is on the East Malaysian coast, where turtles gather to breed, that the dilemma reaches its tragic, brutal climax.

Winner of the 1981 Age Book of the Year, the P.E.N. Golden Jubilee Award, the 1981 Braille Book of the Year, and the 1982 South Australian Government's Biennial Award for Literature.

Monkeys in the Dark

Blanche d'Alpuget

Young Australian journalist Alexandra Wheatfield takes a job in Djakarta at a time of chaotic change: President Sukarno is about to be overthrown, and he has warned the people that without him they are like 'monkeys in the dark'.

Alexandra is moved by the raw colour and sullen violence of life in the city, and it mirrors her affair with Maruli Hutabarat, poet and party activist. But she is faced with the conflicting demands of two societies — her own and that of her lover — and she is finally betrayed by both.

'd'Alpuget's Jakarta is a tense, uneasy place and Alexandra's involvement with a political activist and Indonesian creates a conflict which mirrors the much larger conflict around her.'

Australian

'The poverty, cruelty, insecurity and intrigue of life in the decaying capital [of Jakarta] are made intensely vivid.'

British Book News